Down and Out
Book 1
of
The Undercity Series
by Kris Moger

Juliette Publications

juliettestudios.com

This book is dedicated to my partner in art, Aline; my partner in life, Loni; and my partner in mischief, J.J.

Looking for more from Kris Moger?
Check out:
Outside In (Undercity Book 2) :
The chaos continues.

Taeowolf
In the mist, reality is subjective.
In the mist, there is power.

Chapter 1

The page stared at Teddy, and he glared back as the thoughts in his head abandoned him for a more creative brain. He groaned and rubbed the sore muscles in his neck. After a day of digging, writing was supposed to be fun and relaxing.

Yeah, right. The blank sheet mocked him. Well, sort of blank aside from a row of faded images, the lingering little hints of a past well gone. He drew his tin lamp closer though the stench of the rancid oil wasn't pleasant. Tipping his page toward the flame, he studied the words to decipher what they might mean.

'No, 051-red and b ue – 200 pie es'

Disappointed, he frowned—some inventory list, not interesting. Still, paper was hard enough to come by so he didn't complain. Luck helped him find the box filled to overflowing with lots of usable sheets on their last hunt earlier in the day. His father said anything marked re-cyclables had no value, so he collected enough to share with his sister and keep him writing for a while. One of the best parts of his job as a junk hunter was keeping what his father did not think would sell.

He scribbled, 'It was a dark and stormy night,' and paused, making a face. What did he know about stormy nights? Dark he got; it haunted every corner of his existence and lurked down every hall and tunnel—a monstrous snake ready to devour him if he lost his little flickering light.

Storms were something else. He heard of them while listening in on conversations when Upperlords visited the warehouse and read about them in pieces of books he and his siblings found on scrounging rounds. They were meaningless words like menacing slate clouds and flashes of lightning, which stimulated his curiosity and made him wonder.

Did a person write journals about their lives or what they wanted? His days were an endless journey searching through rubble for sellable items. Dull stuff. Storms and adventures—things he ached to experience.

A year ago the school area collapsed, killing several people, including his teacher, and ending the education of Underlings. He remembered his teacher as relatively kind, but impatient, dedicated to the idea that learning to read would save their society. Though his passion was commendable, his nervous drive was unsettling. Many evenings Teddy would find him curled up in a corner with the remains of some book, tears streaming down his face. Why? Teddy never asked.

His mother insisted those kinds of personal questions were rude, and cultured people did not ask them. How they were cultured people existing in their dugout hovel behind the warehouse in the vast maze of Undercity, he could not guess, but his parents both dreamt of finding one special treasure, which would move them up in the world to the city of the Upperlords.

"A dark and st... st... stormy night?" said Jolon as Teddy realized his brother stood behind him peering over his shoulder. "What kind of way is that to start a story?"

Plopping down on a semi-useable armchair by the makeshift desk, he played with a little box in his hand. He loved to collect all kinds of insects and carried about tiny plastic containers to keep them in. Ma came up with a way for him to display them with pins on a board in his room instead of piled all over.

"Kind of dull... not up to your usual goods."

"This is a journal, Jolon, not a story, and not meant for anyone else to read except me."

"Selfish." His ink black hair kept falling over his mud brown eyes; he wrapped a curl around his pudgy forefinger and tugged. "Deb and Caden ain't gonna be happy either. You know they live for your stories."

Chewing on his lower lip, Teddy massaged his temples and tried to stay calm. After a tedious day of searching through ruins with his siblings yapping in his ear every moment, he yearned for peace and to lose himself in his own world. Though, as Caden came into the room and sprawled her long frame across his bed, he decided there was little chance of that happening. He took a deep breath and reminded himself of how life was before the Petersons adopted him—the solitary nights scrounging for food, the ache for company. The emptiness still lingered even after many years.

He remembered his own parents. At least, he remembered flashes of them—his mom, tawny with a limp and a generous, weary smile, his dad, short and bony with a pug nose and shabby plastic-black hair, which went with a ready laugh and soft-lidded brown eyes. Teddy was a combination of them and often peered in any reflective surface to visualize their faces. His complexion had more of a khaki tone like his father, but he liked the fact that his grin resembled his mother's. He didn't remember how old he was when they went out to scrounge, as most Underlings do, and didn't come back. Nor did he have any idea how many days he lived on his own. Life was a blur of survival and confusion until he lost track of everything nearing normal. Reading was his only escape, his lasting gift from his parents.

When the Petersons found him reading scraps of a book in a corner, Mr. Peterson, or Pa as he called him now, greeted him with a grin distorted by a jagged scar down the side of his face and across his upper lip. At first, Teddy wanted to scurry away and hide as he did whenever someone new came close. But, his soon to be Mother wrinkled her nose and offered a cookie, making such a funny face under her pile of frizzy pale hair he smiled and let them approach, hunger weakening his survival instincts. Both were as pasty in complexion as the gypsum boards, which made up most of the broken walls in Undercity. As he munched their offering, Pa talked to him about books and such until Teddy's fears eased and the Petersons became the first people he trusted since his parents disappeared.

They were kind people. Not too many Underlings assist the various orphans hiding in the passages and tunnels of their world. When he was well into ten years of his life, they gave him a home. Two months later a younger, scrawnier Jolon, now pudgy, with coppery skin prone to pimples and scabs, joined them. His older sister, Caden, already lived with them when he showed up. At first, they each kept their distance from the other, but they came to build a certain level of trust though she still hid much of herself away. Age was irrelevant to most Underlings. Though he knew Deb was seven because he was present when she was born. Although she was the Peterson's only biological child, they treated all their children the same. Everyone adored Deb, even Caden who refrained from affection toward anyone.

"Got some paper for you," he told Caden, and she almost smiled.

She tugged off her mismatched, weathered socks and plucked at the holes in her jeans. He passed her a couple of sheets and a pencil, and she settled into drawing Jolon's portrait.

"So, somebody tell me something interesting," she said in a gruff whisper. Though tall, she carried little meat on her bones and had peeling splotches on her sepia skin.

One thing about the Underworld life was everyone had a sickly greenish-grey tinge to the complexion no matter what the natural colour. If the toxins in the water didn't mutate you, the piped in air did; or the scraps of food grown under fluorescent lamps in exhausted, chemical-soaked soil altered your genes.

"He's writing in a journal, and we don't get to read it."

"Don't be so dramatic." He threw a wad of paper at Jolon.

Caden shrugged as though she didn't care. "So? Can't read, anyway."

"I told you I would help you." He could not resist offering.

She narrowed her gaze. "Don't want help, just want stories. The reading thing is for freaks such as you."

"I can read," Jolon said.

"You stutter and stumble over the words, makes the story weird."

"It's not my fault the letters are all backwards." He stuffed a dry cookie in his mouth.

"That's dyslexia." They didn't seem impressed, and Teddy felt his cheeks flush. "It's true. I read it in a scrap of a book I found in the ruins of one of those office rooms."

Caden shook her head and flopped back on the bed, staring at the wall. "You gotta do that, don't ya—name everything. Who cares? Things are what they are."

"Knowledge is important," he insisted, wishing they understood.

"Uh huh, and here most everyone thought food and water were important." She clicked her tongue and jabbed at his papers. "So, how does it start?"

"What?"

"Your journal."

"A dark and sticky night," Jolon said.

"Stormy. Journals are not for sharing."

"What's a stormy night?" Deb asked as she joined them after finishing her usual play date with their father.

Teddy groaned; he was never going to find any privacy. "Ah…" He stopped, how did a person explain something he only read about. The papers they found in almost every building talked about something called weather, but it seemed obscure. "It has something to do with clouds and sunlight and rain."

"I heard about them," Jolon said, bouncing up and down on his chair while Deb climbed on Teddy's lap.

Her worn pink skirt had new blue patches sewn over the holes, which made her soft blue eyes more intense. Her pastel gold hair frizzed like their mom's and tickled his chin.

Caden scrunched up her nose. "You heard nothin'."

"No, I did, honest. When I went to Market Quarter with Pa last week," he insisted. "This group of Uppers went on about building a new garden with this glass dome thing..."

"Jolon, you're babbling."

"Let him finish," Teddy said, always curious about the Uppercity. Aside from the Theater Quarter, he had been to the market and lived through one horrible encounter in the seedy Adult Quarter, but the rest had always been forbidden, and his brain hungered for details, even made up ones.

"They said they saw this bright sun thing and all this..." His brother faded out as though unable to find the words to describe what he heard.

He leaned back and let his imagination fill in the blanks.

"Teddy, Ma says you need to tell me a story," his little sister informed him with her most serious tone, her intense eyes stared at him.

He smiled and got off his chair, taking her with him as he went. "I need to, huh?"

"Yes, you will shrivel up and turn to dust if you don't," Caden muttered as she fluffed her pillow into submission.

"Oooh, another story?" He tossed his little sister onto the bed. "Ahhh, I guess I can manage that."

Caden took Deb and scooted over while he stretched his legs out and got comfortable beside them. Jolon snuggled into the puffed up chair, and they got cozy. The constant faint hum of the air circulation system soothed their weary bodies much as Teddy imagined a stream of water would.

His brother yawned and tucked his hands under his head. "Don't start with any stormy dark nights. At least, no dark; get enough in the day. Sumpin' bright, 'n daring."

"An' romantic," Deb chipped in while Caden groaned.

"Please, no more mushy junk. It's pathetic."

"Thanks a lot, Cad. If you don't like my adventures, don't listen."

"Nah, I like your stories, it's..." She made a face at him over Deb's head. "Well, ya got the imagination to do storms and such an' make them interesting, but the romance stuff...."

He glared at her. "Yes?"

"Well, it's all kinda; I don't know, if that's romance, I don't want any." She rolled to her stomach, her face unreadable.

Teddy studied her, suspecting something more to what she claimed, but he let it go. They both realized a while back any discussions about anything personal had to happen in a more private setting; otherwise, every subject became a family topic and led to endless embarrassment.

"Fine," he said with a tang of bitterness and settled into his tale.

The next morning, Teddy was stiff and sore with what felt like a permanent hollow in his side where Deb's elbow spent the night. Since sunlight never touched any area of Undercity, they set their time by a pendulum clock, which stood in the centre courtyard of Uppercity where people gathered to socialize and trade with each other. The Upperlords determined the accuracy of this timepiece, and they judged their time by the position of the sun travelling over the greenhouses.

The chimes from the windup clock in the kitchen rang out with its whirring metallic bell; he rolled off the edge of his bed and stood, stretching. One of his parents must have come in and blew out the flame in the night, so the room was black. He patted the shelf by his bed until he found his tiny handlight and flicked it on long enough to light his tin and rag lamp again. The armchair lacked an occupant, and he decided his brother vacated to his own bed sometime in the night.

"Come on, let's get breakfast before Jolon eats everything," he said, scratching his head, the strands of hair greasy. Well, two more days to bathing day. He sniffed and decided by the musty strong odour in the room it couldn't come too soon.

Caden twisted out of the blankets. "Ohhhahhhggg, yeah, yeah, I'm coming." As she sat up, she wove her fingers in her curls. "Eh, perfect."

"Problem?"

"Just the usual hair issues. Serves me right. Went to bed without covering it. Never good."

The whiff of potatocakes drifted in, and Deb went from inert to almost bouncing out of the room with a loud yell of "Foooooooood."

Teddy laughed as he placed his lamp in a larger can and picked the holder up by the wire handle on the side. The makeshift lantern wasn't the easiest thing to carry, but the flame kept the gloom back.

"Oh, help, she takes way too much energy." His sister got up and patted his head as she left the room, her daily reminder she stood at least six inches above him.

He ignored her and wandered down the narrow hall. The icy cement nipped his bare feet and sent a chill up his spine. He entered the kitchen where warmth radiated from the stove—a sizeable metal tank their father made up and piped to vent the smoke. The cooker worked most of the time, his father being quite handy and resourceful. Sometimes his resourcefulness earned the favour of several Upperlords and provided the family with such luxuries as direct vents to the main purifier instead of recycled air. Teddy didn't want to be negative about the community he lived in, but most people seemed to possess a high level of acceptance and lack of hunger for a society with little food and terrible living conditions.

Overall, their home was small and somewhat dilapidated, but the place was security to Teddy. He loved every corner even when washing day was a ways away and the dishes piled high in their bin.

"Oh, my loves," their mother greeted with her hair everywhere and a wave of a half leg from a wooden chair. She turned and opened the stove door, shoving the wood in.

"Cakes are up and syrup is..." She squinted at the label on the jar. "Grape, I think." She stuck a finger in and licked the digit spotless. "Still tastes good, though. Who wants some?"

Deb jumped up and down. "Me, me, me."

Teddy added his lamp to the two on their rickety, stained plastic table, snatched a potatocake from the tray, and slathered jam all over the patty before curling it up and handing the roll, plateless to save water, to his sister. She snickered and shoved half in her mouth, her cheeks bulging.

Pa sat down on his stool and stuck his legs out in front of him. "Well, all Upper orders are filled and yesterday's haul should satisfy any new inquiries for a while. Seems as though we've got a fragment of breathing space." He beamed, excitement sparkling in his pale blue eyes. "So, I figure we dig through the southern corridor today." He winked and scratched at his patchy beard. "Might be the big one. Promising, eh, Teddy?"

He swallowed hard as his father's plan stirred a thrill in his chest. "Yep, 'cording to the map."

"If you can trust a wilted book with odd pages and weird pictures," Caden mumbled as she picked at a potatocake.

"Hey, that was one of my best finds," Jolon protested, his fists full of food.

Pa grasped Jolon's shoulder as he bounced to his feet. "Hasn't failed us yet. Whelp, let's get moving, my gophers. Who can tell what kinds of things we will find today?"

"But I'm not done."

Ma fluffed Jolon's curls. "Rest easy, dear, I want you to stay and help me and Deb transform yesterday's booty." She held out a thermos and a couple of packs of potatocakes and cookies. "Don't forget these and tell your pa oil stocks are getting low so we might need to change to the gas torches if you can't find any."

Teddy stuffed the supplies in his survival stash before he slung the grey sack over his shoulders and adjusted the straps. He rushed after his father and sister while Deb shrieked with delight and his brother groaned, muttering complaints about having to do all the disgusting work.

They entered the shadowy warehouse and collected their scrounging gear. Boxes, bags, and piles filled every corner in an ordered system only his mother understood. Their home was a secure fortress surrounded by cement walls and metal fences with a bridge across a broad crevice, isolating them from the worst of Undercity's dangers. Sometimes rival scroungers would try to break in, but never succeeded.

They did not make enough money to hire a brute, which the more respectable places owned, so they made do with two mangy dogs who slept most of the time. Critter was a huge, rugged creature more vicious in appearance than in nature, and Stub was, well, a tiny three-legged thing nastier than she appeared. Teddy didn't carry much love for either of them, they stunk and drooled.

"Now," his father began as they made their way through the cluttered racks, "I'm guessing we follow this staircase a while further. I don't want you two to be nervous, but I'm not too certain where we are going." He whistled and Critter came loping over, nails clicking on the cement, with Stub marching behind.

"What do you mean?" asked Teddy, exchanging puzzled glances with Caden. "I thought the map was pretty clear."

He gave the dogs their breakfast, which they gulped and slurped faster than he poured the goopy leftovers into their bowl. "It is, but we're heading into the more central part of the old city. We should locate lots of shops and other places to plunder, but we might find a higher concentration of..." He paused to put his effort into moving the wood and steel door hiding their access to the tunnels. The metal screeched and creaked, screaming in protest as the bottom scraped against cement. They helped, shoving with everything they had.

Pa huffed and cracked a wacky grin. He left the remainder of his last sentence behind and hoisted his bulging stash to his back. Teddy snatched up the lantern Ma created from little candles, jars, and wire. They worked where they had air. By doing so, they saved their hand-lights and batteries for the dead spaces.

A shiver trickled down his spine as it did when he explored the passages of the past. It was staggering to consider the many places they scrounged were once outside, exposed to the elements.

According to his schooling, history's leaders had foreseen the vast meteor shower, which decimated their world. To prepare, they built an immense dome out of some advanced energy network they created in outer space. What they did not predict was the massive seismic backlash. Extensive sections of the protective net collapsed leaving only a small portion to live in thus creating Uppercity.

Still, he had a home, a family, and a means of making credits. Not much to some and luxury to others, but safe to them.

At first, the area was essentially impassable with rubble and garbage, but they were experts at dealing with such obstacles. Though the work was hard, they spent over a year cleaning them out and achieved much with few resources. Now, the passages were comfortable to travel.

The roof was good. Only three places sustained major damage and needed re-enforcing with beams and whatever else they scrounged up. They found few corpses along the way and those had decayed to skeletons. Those they disposed of with as much dignity as they could, sealing them up whenever they came to a little hovel leading nowhere else.

A scurrying, scratching sound echoed down the hall; they froze, waiting for more. Teddy gripped the blade he'd strapped to his side, searching for mutated rat dogs, crazed, vicious creatures, which lurked in the gaps and shadows. After one tried to rip his arm off, he always kept a sharp knife on him. His father was adept at killing the things though the scar on his face served as a reminder to them not to get overconfident.

"Might be shifting rubble," Caden said with hope in her voice.

They waited a moment, but nothing happened. Pa sheathed his blade and agreed. "I guess all is clear. Go forth, gophers, go."

Exhaling, Teddy let himself breathe again. He exchanged a grimace with her and caught up with their father.

"If we can discover one thing, that one amazing thing, we might move up and enjoy the sky," Pa said.

He was a dreamer and Teddy understood because a day didn't go by when he did not fantasize the same thing.

Caden rolled her amber eyes. "Yeah, yeah. The skies will part and the world will shift, and yada, yada, yada."

He gave her a half hug. "Oh, come now, my pessimist, find hope and bring a smile to your beautiful face."

She hid behind her hair, struggling with her difficulties with self-esteem. Teddy had seen her stare in mirrors and turn away in disgust.

Somehow, Pa had a healing effect on her. He was not so handsome with his scar, kinked back, and twisted leg, which made his toes point to the side. Perhaps the twinkle in his eyes and his addictive personality gave her comfort. His presence always improved Teddy's mood.

"Dream with me, girl. Keep me young."

Caden managed one of her rare smiles. "Fine," she said with more affection than usual. "Oh, wow, wouldn't it be wonderful?"

Teddy shared a chuckle with his father who lifted his lantern, casting light far along the corridor.

"It'll do."

"Don't say anything," she said as Pa guided them. "He's happy, that's what counts."

"Okay," he said and scrubbed his jaw to hide a smile though he understood his sister's wariness.

She punched his arm. "Oh, stop."

He could only imagine what her life was like in the Nest, the home of the traffickers who sold people to Adult Quarter scum of Uppercity. Some became brutes, some slaves, and others adult amusement. At least, that was a fate he avoided growing up. Every time he passed those seedier markets, he felt as though a thousand covetous eyes trailed after him. Eligible, desirable bodies were rare commodities Uppers valued, which was why their little sister never left their home. His parents itched to move up from the sewers to improve their daily comfort and for their protection.

'A brute; this is what they need,' his father would say and hug Deb close as she grew older. Apprehension showed in his eyes, so they all watched over her.

Teddy coughed as they reached a pocket of sour air. They slipped on masks and breathed in some oxygen from their tanks attached to their stash packs. It was not much, and they handled them with care, but the equipment allowed them to pass through various gas pockets and dead spots. They flicked on their handlights as their candles went out. Soon, they would reach the area where the passage would open up into a larger space. They stepped into the echoing chamber.

Caden shone her light toward the roof. "Hey, Teddy, if we can breathe the air filtering down from above, why can't we dig our way to the surface and leave this city behind?"

He shrugged. "I think it involves the strength of the rays and the violence of the storms raging on the sun. At least, that's what my teacher used to say."

"Hm." She picked her way through the rubble. "The school thing didn't give many answers, did it? Seemed to make more questions."

He shrugged again. "They tried. Too bad you never went."

"Yeah, well, the whole thing's a vast pit now, isn't it? No teachers, no books, just a hole leading to an even deeper hole."

"Would you have liked to have gone?"

She kept her eyes on their father who was several feet in front of them. "I guess. Hey, Pa, are we going to go all day or do we get to stop and snack on something?"

He dropped his stash on the ground and sat down on the crumbled cement. "Good idea. Bring out the goodies."

A while later, after they munched a potato pie and had a drink, they proceeded down another corridor and roamed the twists and turns, which terminated at a concrete staircase. Most times, they avoided stairs because they tended to be unsafe and often led nowhere. This particular set had a few cracks in the steps' treads and risers but seemed sound enough.

"How far did we get last time?"

"One flight," Teddy answered.

"Oh, yeah, Jolon tripped over his two klutzy feet and tumbled back down," Caden whacked Pa on his shoulder. "Good idea leaving him home this time."

"Now, Cad, it's not his fault his one leg is shorter than the other."

"Ah, huh, makes him unstable, I know, poor thing," she said and went forward.

Teddy ignored his sister's lack of sympathy and went with her up the steps. Their candles cast little light, and the gloom of the tunnels was unsettling. Bits of gravel and rubble made the stairs slippery as rocks stuck in the treads of his boots. Alert for danger, they all kept silent though the sound of their crunching of feet bounced around them.

At the top of the first flight, their father moved in front, beads of sweat trickling down his face. Teddy paused and took a drink from his flask. The air was hot and thin, making him somewhat lightheaded. He inhaled a long breath and trailed after Caden. More debris covered the second level, and they tread with care in case it hid weaknesses, which might cause the whole staircase to fall apart.

The third landing was almost impassable. The outer wall had collapsed into a heaping mass of rubble and twisted metal. Teddy inched onto part of the pile, holding his light high.

"Not much here, but broken cement and such. No way through, either. Not without an extensive excavation," he told them as he came back to the steps.

After handing his lantern to Caden, their father took out his map, turning it about to find their location. He tapped the paper with a finger.

"Appears as though this doesn't lead to much." He peered further up the staircase. "There's more up this way if this thing is accurate."

Teddy frowned. "Pa, half of this is missing. How are we gonna get up to the next level?"

"There's always a way, boy. We always find a way." He put on his playful and infuriating grin.

Caden snorted in exasperation. "Remember, Ma will kill you if we come back in pieces."

"We've always gotten back, yes?" he said with a laugh.

"Yeah, sort of and not always without wounds."

"This debris contains some metal," Pa said as he crammed the map back in the front pocket of his grey stash, pulled out a folding shovel, and began to dig. "Let's check if anything can help us."

Shaking his head, Teddy propped his lantern on a step and took out some gloves. "You wanna toss this rubbish downward?"

"Best way to remove the stuff. Stay clear of the stairs. Don't want to block our way down."

"Yeah, that would be peachy," said Caden as she lobbed a slab of crumbling wall over the railing. It fell into the black void and hit the bottom with a clang. The noise echoed around them.

Teddy grabbed a bent metal sign and shovelled rubble over the edge. Dust and dirt whirled around them, forcing them to wear the respirators they kept in their packs. After what seemed to be hours, he rested, coughing as he sipped some water.

They cleared a fair portion of space on the narrow cement landing, enough for them to continue upward. Weary, they all put away their masks and took a thirst-quenching drink. Pa studied the next flight of stairs as they rested.

"These break off half way. If we can stretch these steel braces across, we might make our way up."

Exchanging a fatigued glance with Caden, Teddy rubbed at his forehead before assisting his father as he hoisted one of the warped metal beams upward. He grunted, his arms straining under the weight, but they maneuvered the girder across the gap in the steps.

Pa huffed as he pushed at the beam. "Well, I don't think we're gonna move this any further without help." He began to climb the slender bridge, holding tight to the edges and gripping with his toes. Teddy moved in behind him to be able to catch him in case he fell.

After a few precarious moments, his father stood on the lip of the next landing. "Okay, I'm up." He pulled out his handlight and swept the beam about. "All appears good from here. Not too much rubble." He set his light aside. Kneeling, he held out his hands. "Cad, you next."

She frowned and put down her lantern before starting to climb. "If I fall, I will blame you for the rest of your life."

Teddy steadied her from behind. "Me? I'm not the one who came up with this silly idea."

Her foot slipped as she hit the halfway point and she yelped, but their father leaned down and seized her hand.

"I got you."

She muttered something incoherent as she passed him and crawled to a safe spot near the landing's back wall.

Pa tilted his body toward Teddy. "Hand me the lights."

He passed each one up before climbing. His fingers gripped the edges of the girder as he willed his feet to stick to the metal. Breath shallow and nerves taunt, he climbed beside his father. He blew the hair from his eyes and tightened his jaw as he peeked downward.

"The journey back is going to be a bugger, isn't it?"

"Eh, we'll tackle that later. For the moment, up, up we go."

Caden grabbed a lantern and inched her way toward the top. Pa whistled as he climbed as though going for a leisurely stroll. Teddy trailed after them, and they ascended two more flights. They stopped at the last landing.

Filthy glass double doors, which begged to be opened, stood at the other end. This was what he loved about scrounging, finding a new area, discovering how life once was. He wiped away some of the dirt to reveal a plastic film with coloured images blocking his view.

"Masks on," Pa said, taking the precaution that shielded them from any toxic gasses lurking behind the sealed entrance.

In one sense, he didn't need to fear, at least not for Teddy. He had his breath caught in the knots in his stomach. His father tossed a crowbar his way and put another one to the seam between the doors. Together, they forced the panels apart an inch. Caden leaned in, peering through the opening before she shook her head. Trading a glance with Pa, he nodded. They tried again, putting all their effort into it.

Teddy grunted through his mask as he flexed and strained his body. "Can't we just break the glass?"

"That would be cheating," Pa said with a snicker.

She scrunched her nose. "Yes, let's be fair to the inert piece of hardware blocking our way."

The doors creaked open inch-by-inch until she could hold her lantern high and let the light through. A soft wind blew at her hair as the air escaped. Pa and Teddy waited, but she backed away. They went at it again. This time, the two of them grasped one frame and heaved until they had space to go through.

Panting, they wiped the sweat from their faces, Teddy's excitement mirrored in his father's eyes. He grinned, gesturing to Teddy to go first. His hand shook as he held his lantern high, hoping for safe passage into the unknown.

At first, he saw little, just another room. Slowly, he realized it was a foyer with another intact pair of clear doors several feet beyond. Dust and cobwebs covered the area; otherwise, the place was clean of debris. He stepped forward with his sister and his father behind him. The glass was cold against his fingers, and their lights reflected off the surface, showing them distorted pictures of themselves. His father took hold of one of the handles and pulled. The door swung open and another gust, stronger than the last, rushed past them.

Teddy slung his stash off and took out his portable air tester. He pressed a button and hoped the batteries were still good. While his father always made certain their equipment worked in top order, working batteries were a rarity. The lights came on. Green. Good, breathable oxygen levels. He gestured a thumb's up to his father and sister and took his foggy mask off. A tingle of fear and doubt touched him as he hesitated before taking his first breath. It was the same sensation he always experienced and shared with the others when experiencing the unknown of a new region. He inhaled stale, but breathable, air with a metallic flavour. Relieved, the three of them laughed.

"Amazing how spotless this area is," Teddy said, scanning the space with his light.

Caden put her fingers on the next entrance, staring through the glass. "It's weird how some areas are rubble and some are almost pristine. Looks like a solid barricade of crap and dirt this way."

"Must be something about the way they're built," Pa said, searching his supplies.

"There's another room over here." Teddy crossed to the wall on the right and tapped on a set of smooth tan doors. The metallic sound echoed through the room. "Huh, elevator?"

"I'd say so."

"Got a single door over here." Caden placed a hand on the silver bar across it.

"Just wait," their father cautioned. "We've gone far enough for today. Let's see if we can figure out where we are." He sat down on a stone bench near the wall to their left. She held her light over the book in his hand as he flipped the pages to discover where they were. "Mon... Montgom...."

"Montgomery Mall," Teddy said. "Ummm." He turned toward the others and pointed at the words carved above the trim. "East entrance."

"What's a mall?" asked Caden and Pa laughed.

Chapter 2

Pa bounced around like a child with a cookie. He would not hold still. The instant they returned from scrounging, he swept their mother in his arms and twirled her around. "We did it; we did it!"

His enthusiasm was contagious and sent everyone dancing around the table even though they didn't know why. Deb shouted and spun about, and even Jolon cheered. They all celebrated except Caden, who stood by the door with her arms crossed, her face puzzled and cautious.

"Did what?" she asked. "All I saw was yet another building. The only good thing about it seemed to be the lack of junk."

Pa waved a finger at her. "Ahh, but the magic exists in the contents of the mall."

She traded an uncertain glance with Teddy, and somehow he got the message.

"What's that?" he asked her.

Their father sighed and settled himself on his stool, reclining against the wall as he stretched out his legs. Deb crawled on his lap, staring into his eyes. He touched her hair.

"Oh, everything you might think of. Your grandfather told me the stories your great-grandfather told him about these places similar to our markets only bigger—dozens of stores selling hundreds of thousands, millions of items—clothes, dishes, batteries—whatever you could imagine, and it's all waiting for us to find." "If the stuff isn't all trash by now," Caden said.

"Oh, no." Pa smiled. "This is our moment. After so many years, this is our moment. Some of what we find may be use- less, I'll admit, but there must be so much more." He leaned forward, hugging Deb. "You understand what this means?"

Ma studied him, her hands on her hips as though bracing for his latest endeavour. "What are you thinking now, Truman, dear?"

He gave a wicked grin. "It's time. It's time."

"Time for what?" asked Jolon.

"Oh, please. Tell us," Caden demanded as he paused and winked.

He tweaked Deb's nose. "It's time we got ourselves a brute. Yes, that's the next step."

Ma's face mixed with fear, disbelief, and hope. "Oh, Tru."

Teddy traded glances with his family, anticipation running through everyone and questions poured forth like the candy from a broken gumball machine.

"Where do we get one?"

"What are they like?"

"Does it have to live here? I'm not sharing my bed."

That was Jolon and his practical nature. Teddy shoved him.

"What? It might stink."

"Brutes aren't an it; they're people like us." He glanced over at Pa, feeling a twinge of doubt. "Right?"

His father ruffled Teddy's hair. "You'll get to decide for yourself when we go up."

He grinned even though his insides turned knots at the thought of getting to be a part of the purchase. All the rest of the day he flipped from excitement to dread, his mind active with scenarios ranging from happy-ever-after to doom and destruction. Sleep was a fitful friend who refused to linger and so when morning came, he sat near the kitchen table and waited.

He fidgeted with a little plastic box his mother kept spoons in. His parents were awake; he heard them moving around in their bedroom right next door. Yawning, he listened in on their conversation.

"Must we take Teddy with us?" his mother asked.

"Yes," Pa answered with his 'don't worry' voice.

"But...."

"No, dear, I understand. The danger is real, but the boy must learn, he must make contacts. He's old enough now, and Caden isn't ever going to be strong enough."

"She's bold enough in spirit."

"Yes, but if anything happened to...." His father paused.

"Dear, you're...."

Their door opened, and she closed her mouth, ending their conversation as she caught sight of Teddy.

"Well, ready to go?" Pa's voice was cheerful, but his face unreadable.

Teddy acted as though he had not heard them. "All set."

Ma gave a trace of an anxious smile as she pushed her hair out of her face and went to the cupboard.

"Good. A helping of breakfast and off we go," his father said with a wink. He sat and began sorting through some papers.

Teddy waited, but if they wanted to share any concerns with him, they didn't give any indications. After eating his food in silence, he followed them out.

When they first stepped from the service lift connecting Uppercity and Undercity together, the sheer intensity of the place made his heart beat faster. The air was thinner, fresher while strange lights filtered down from half-covered windows high above. He wanted to get a glimpse of what lay beyond them, but the glass was all too murky and dim.

A constant, annoying whirring pulsed under the clamour of people, reminding everyone their source of power belonged in the control of the Magistrate and the generators ran as long as they all behaved. It was an effective way to ensure a law- abiding society. Darkness was rare, relegated to corners where the streetlights didn't reach. He wondered what made them glow. The streets were clean too, tidied every night by Underlings paid in rotting vegetables and ragged clothing, and whatever castoffs they deemed as salvageable.

It made him sad, the contrast between those above and those below. What made them so special they could be so greedy? The answer lay all around him. They had the food and the air. They controlled access to all their basic needs, even water, which came in drips and drabs and weekly doses. Nothing made sense.

The three of them left the general market area and turned down the avenue leading to the central sections of Uppercity. He frowned as the Upperlords meandered by with their immaculate clothes and fresh faces. They didn't appear pale or gaunt. Suffering did not haunt their bodies like a sickly grey aura smothering hope. They were straight and healthy as they received the best of the supplies and services, leaving the leftovers to the Underlings.

Still, what could Unders do? They had the brutes, and no Underling could afford one. It was where the strong and powerful went to survive. They became the controlling force for the Upperlords who housed, clothed, and fed as many as a dozen depending on how extensive their riches and property. The most affluent ran the greenhouses, and water and air supplies. Some owned land and shelter while others bought clothing and various items from Underlings like his father and supplied them for those above. Every one of them kept at least one brute— giant, muscular people who had no emotion or boundaries as to what they were willing to do—and his father buying one.

"Pa, are you sure we need one of those?" he asked as they wandered past two bookend walls of muscle protecting the elaborate entrance to a grand and imposing building. They glared hatred at him as he and his parents went, their eyes black and faces scarred.

His father took Ma's hand. "Don't stress. We'll find one just right for us."

She didn't seem convinced. Blinking in the light, she appeared diminished, which was strange to witness. In their home, she filled the room though she stood two inches shorter than Pa. Here, her smile hid, and her usual dancing eyes held fear. Her timid manner unnerved him. She did not like Uppercity, but she would not let their father go to the market to buy a brute without her. In their home and their warehouse, she controlled everything.

The Uppers understood when they visited and treated her with respect. Now, he realized they faked deference to her. Up here, they gazed through her as though she was nothing, and this added to the anger burning in him like a child wanting life to be fair. It wasn't happening, he got that, but it did not mean he could stop himself from being angry.

"Calm yourself, love. They can sense despair," his mother said with a playful wink though tension lingered about her mouth. "Don't take everything so personal. They live their lives, and we go on with ours. To be honest, I think ours is better." She raised a hand to shield her eyes as she gazed up at the vaulted ceiling several stories above their heads. "I must admit I would love to see so much space every day."

"Ma, do you think Pa should get a brute before we even make sure we've found anything interesting? I mean, they are expensive, aren't they?"

She patted his hand and gripped his palm. "Rest easy. I have confidence in your father's instincts; I always have and always will. If I didn't, I wouldn't live the life I do. I wouldn't have your brother and sisters, or you. So, we trust him." Her smile turned into a grim line as they went through the arches and entered the Market Quarter. "Besides, they can't all be expensive."

Teddy hoped she was right. He gazed around at all the stalls where many of the vendors sold wares his family scrounged up. Every booth cried out opulence and ownership. People flocked to them, haggling with goods of their own or papers of credit for items from other shops. Upper Market was a strange chess game where nothing was worth anything and everything cost something. What else was there to do, but collect things from a dead society?

He took a deep breath as they moved closer to the Adult Quarter. Sometimes, he, Caden, and Jolon would get a couple of cheap credits each to go to one of the plays or concerts in the Theater Quarter with strict instructions to keep to the children's shows. This was a straightforward rule for Teddy. A year before he met his family, he took a wrong path and got lost in the Nest's maze of tiny rooms. He made his escape with sheer luck and a slight build, which enabled him to hide in crevices, but not before getting an unwanted glimpse of the Uppercity escort auction house. Now, every time he went near either area he shuddered and stayed close to his father. Once, Jolon wanted to explore the slum, but he was too scared to go alone. Caden had her reasons for staying away. Teddy never asked for details; he didn't need to. They shared a glance, and that was enough.

Sometimes, Pa would leave them at the theater and go chat with his friendlier contacts. Occasionally, Ma joined him, but she preferred shopping for fresh food they could not grow or raise such as eggs or vegetables.

As they left the quarter behind, Teddy recognized a few Under creepers lurking about. The sight of them made him shiver. They were the worst kind of desperate, willing to search through the poor and suffering of Undercity for anyone they could sell. Too many Underlings disappeared due to them. One, a short, stubby man with too much hair and not enough teeth, scanned Teddy over in a way that made him ill. Another man joined him, and they leaned close, whispering and giving him disturbing side-glances.

The other man was a slimy, narrow character named Dorkas who liked to dig into trouble. He was a pale sort with knobby knees and a long face. Sometimes Pa ended up in heated, pointless discussions with him. He hated the shifty creeper who lingered around where no one wanted him.

They worked their way through the crowds until they came to a platform at the end of the market. Two people sat on high-backed chairs with dull velvet upholstery as though they were royalty from his books of old. Both had an ink-black complexion deeper than Jolon or even Caden, more smooth and pure than he had ever seen before.

One woman was all angles with long hair twisted into tight braids and streaked grey and black. She slouched in her seat, chewing on a crooked carrot with the air of someone running out of entertainment options.

Her companion was stubby and turnip-shaped with gold eyes. She had painted lips and wiry hair knotted in a whirling, plaited bun atop her head. Unlike the other, her midnight blue suit was clean, crisp, and appeared as though sewn on her. Despite her neat appearance, something about her demeanor made him uncomfortable. She had a way of looking at a person as though calculating just how much profit she might make from them. The way she scanned his body made him slip behind his father and grasp his mother's arm.

Pa took her hand. "Ah, Belinda, good to see you."

The blue-suit woman raised a thick eyebrow and snapped a crisp nod.

"Truman!" cried the other woman, sitting up in her chair and tossing her carrot aside. "Truman Peterson, someone to brighten my day. Here to peruse the brutes again?"

Pa nodded and grinned. "You remember my wife, Tisha?" He gestured toward Ma who smiled and dipped her head in greeting. "This is my son, Teddy. Teddy, this is Georges and Belinda, sisters and the best brute merchants around."

He was almost certain they were the only brute merchants any-where. His father winked at him, and he decided his father was being political.

"Ah, Tru, being sly again, are ya?" Georges laughed. "Come, let me show you the one singled out for Magistrate Tipins himself."

She led them through a door behind their chairs and through to their inner chambers. Teddy blinked as he tried to keep his eyes from bugging out of his head. Gathered about a colourful square platform were some of the most fearsome looking people he ever saw—brutes of different backgrounds, colours, and shapes—some hairy everywhere, others completely bald. They wore little more than shorts, and many of them bulged out with bulk as though someone overstuffed them until their skin became stretched and thin. Their primary purpose seemed to be the continued lifting of weights and challenging each other to prove who was stronger. He had to admit, they were impressive; his arms were threads in comparison. A massive brute with no hair and scarred streaks through his ash-grey skin stood flexing his skills by seeing just how many other brutes he could lift at once. So far, he held three on a platform above his head. All around, the others laid bets for credits.

"Isn't he amazing? My people found him devouring rats in the sep-tic sewers of South Side. Took five of them to convince him he was bet-ter off coming here."

Pa turned a little pale. "Impressive." He crossed his arms over his chest and chewed his bottom lip. "So, so, tell me, how, how much is... how much does someone such as him cost?"

Georges laughed. "Far more than either of us might scrape up in a lifetime. Still, my sister and I will make a tidy profit, and he will get a better life."

The woman's voice held a genuine note of sorrow, which made Ted-dy think he might like her. She slapped his father on the back and nar-rowed her gold eyes as she studied him.

"I want one," his father said, his voice tight with excitement. "A brute, I want one."

"I know, Tru, you've been coming here for years, and I'd love to give you one... gives a person a boost in society, yes? But they require constant attention and what do you need one for? Yes, you come up with some of the best merchandise the Undercity offers, but your home is a fortress, and those dogs I gave you must offer enough protection. My friend, a brute would only attract scrutiny, unwanted scrutiny." Her voice dipped in volume as she leaned closer to Pa.

Teddy exchanged glances with Ma. Was the Upperlord right? She gave an almost imperceptible shake of her head. He took a slow breath and waited. "I want a brute."

"Tru? You're serious, aren't you? You want... you... a brute. What are you up to? What did you find?"

His father stepped aside to a more secluded corner. "Can't say, yet. It's just its time. That is all I can tell you. Now, do you have one I might afford?"

Georges let out a billowing sigh. "Come on, let's go somewhere a little quieter to talk." She motioned toward a plain wooden door to their left.

Pa donned a cheerful smile and held his arm out for Ma. She placed her hand on his forearm though she passed a doubtful glance to Teddy who fell in behind.

They entered a small room with papers, books, and pictures piled everywhere—on the tables, the floor, two loveseats and the bookshelves. A single light dangled from above.

"Sorry," Georges said, pushing a stack aside and clearing a loveseat for Teddy's parents to sit. "As you know, Tru, I crave literature in any form. I'm afraid I don't possess much of an addiction to," she twitched her shoulders and scanned the room, "tidiness."

They sat down, and Teddy tried to guess her age. Yes, grey streaked her hair, but her sparkling eyes seemed so young. Then again, in this world, it was difficult to tell with anyone. Either way, he figured he might like her.

"Okay, my friend, I've known you for a day past my sanity." She leaned against the corner of a table. "And you and I have done business... well, let's just say you are a man of integrity who leaves the details of our dealings to privacy."

"In other words, he does not tell your sister about your more philanthropic endeavors," Ma interjected. "Nor, should he. It is rare enough to find an Upperlord with any sense of compassion let alone the guts to act even in secret. You are a good woman, Ms. Baldwin."

"True, enough, my lady," she said with a nod. "I appreciate the compliment though I would prefer if you kept your declaration of my mmmm... let's say 'better side' to yourself. I must confess I get uneasy thinking of myself in those terms. I like to keep up my reputation, even with myself. And as you understand, my sister would not want to hear of my weaknesses either. She believes I am uninterested in life, and I prefer to leave it that way... leaves more room for manoeuvrability."

Scratching at the back of her head, she pursed her full lips. "The trick is brutes are a hot commodity. Even the cheap models are quite expensive for you must go through Belinda, and she does not believe in charity." She plucked a pad of paper from a low side table and stared at the first page as though it was the most important thing at the moment.

"However, if you are serious, I do own a brute. Well, sort of, which I might let you purchase. Now mind you, he's green and, well, let's say he possesses potential. He is a good... boy, and he doesn't belong here at all. In fact, Belinda wants me to unload him from our stock, bad for business. I wanted to place him with a friend of his, Kemi or Kemkem, or something like that, but his owner died, and Belinda assigned him to a more secretive location. Apparently, his former owner taught him to read, and she has this fear that thinking will spread and corrupt all her merchandise. So she sticks the smart ones in the darkest holes she can find."

"This brute, he's educated too?" Teddy asked, interested.

She laughed. "In some ways, I guess, but no. He's not too bright or brutish either."

Pa deflated. "He doesn't sound too promising. I was rather hoping to pick up a more, how shall I say, skilled model."

"Yes, but what can you pay with, Tru? Any other must go through my sister. She would insist on full price, which is more credits than you can gather in a year. Now, I wish life was different, but you lack the protection to set up your own booth where you would make the real credits. You and I both understand how ruthless those marketers are. They cut your throat if you fall short in sufficient security."

"So you're damned if you do and you're condemned if you don't," Teddy said.

Georges laughed. "That is one way of putting it. You can't move up in the world if you don't own a grade A brute, and you can't get a high-quality brute if you can't move up in the world and make more credits. Right enough, you are a smart boy."

He squirmed as she studied him.

"Good looking, too. You better hide him. Ole Torod is on the hunt for some fresh blood, according to rumours, and this one fits his bill."

His mother put a protective hand on him. "We keep our children close. They are never out of our sight."

She stood. "Good, good. Well, that puts us back to where we were. How about it? Why not, at least, check out my brute and decide if he will do or not?"

"What grade is he?" Ma asked.

"Hmm?"

"If he is not grade A, what is he? B? C?"

Georges fidgeted with her papers. "The whole grading thing is ugly and unnecessary."

"Show him to us."

The woman pursed her lips and gave a curt nod.

When they got back to their home, Teddy went right into his room and wrote in his journal. 'It was dark and stormy, and I don't think life will get any better. In fact, I predict things will get ugly from here on.' He put his pencil down and thumped his forehead on his desk.

"You keep putting dents in your head, and people will stop thinking you're handsome."

He glared at Caden as she dropped into his overstuffed chair, her chin-length mass of coal black curls and twists caught under a periwinkle scarf and her body wrapped in a speckled green comforter. "Ha, ha. Have you seen him?"

She scratched her head. "Kinda fits this family, I guess. Not much of a brute, though. I mean, he's thick and brawny enough, but not scary. Sorta similar to the oversized fluffy bear we found for Deb's last birthday. I think I can take him in a fight. I think Deb can too, but she fights dirty."

Jolon scrambled in the room, looking back over his shoulder as he went. "Is that it? Is that him? Does he hide secret weapons? I heard they carry secret weapons and such." He tumbled into Caden who pushed him onto the bed.

"If they're secret or hidden, how would we tell? Who is he going to intimidate with a silly expression?"

"Pa says the gentle ones often are meaner than they appear," Teddy said, wishing his father had made another choice.

"It's bad enough we can't afford a brute, but now we've gone beyond scraping the underside of the pit to picking up the slug hiding underneath."

"According to the master of the brutes, he defeated three of the worst Underling gangsters in South Side, but I have my doubts about her honesty."

Caden laughed low. "Yeah, somehow I got a few doubts too."

"Come on. Maybe he's not so bad," Jolon said, his voice cracking with enthusiasm. "I bet he's got those skills, you know, the ones you read to us about in the book, the ningi skills."

"Ninja skills," Teddy corrected his mind elsewhere. "Come on, let's get some supper."

They filed into the kitchen and stared at their new guest. He was massive with shoulders wider than most doorways though only a few inches taller than Pa. He appeared to be in his twenties, which said something for his survival skills since many Underlings only lived to their early teens if left on their own. His dusky brown hair hung down his back while his mold green eyes twinkled with happiness, and his freckled white cheeks flushed. This cast doubts on his bruting expertise, as did his open, honest face, which seemed ready to laugh at anything.

Ma set the food before them. "All right, no staring." They grabbed sandwiches made with fresh potato bread from the market. "And I mean every one of you," she admonished the brute as he kept his eyes stuck on the others. "Children, this is Henri. Henri, this is our eldest daughter, Caden, our boy, Jolon, and you already met our eldest boy, Teddy." She singled each one out in turn.

The brute gave a half toothy grin and a half bow with a shy wave.

"We keep another little troublemaker around here, but she is asleep. Someone decided to play scout with her among the furniture isles." She shook her head at Caden, who studied her sandwich.

Her mouth twisted with mischief. "She had fun."

"Poor thing is all worn out. Now, let's eat and after we'll work on the sleeping arrangements. Your father is securing the warehouse." She brushed Henri's forearm; he froze, blushing. "We'll walk you through everything tomorrow."

Teddy swallowed hard. There was only one place for their brute to stay... with him... in his room... in his sanctuary. His sandwich lost its flavour. Caden shifted her gaze over to him and snickered. He couldn't say anything; she had to share with Deb, and Jolon's room was little more than a closet. Perhaps Henri could use the closet, and he could bunk with Jolon. He eyed his brother as he slurped his way through a sandwich and belch and decided to give the brute a try. Besides, Jolon tended to snore like a dying rat.

He finished his food and gulped down his water. Motioning to Henri, he stood. "Come on. You can share my room," he said with a meaningful glance at his mother.

She messed his hair as he left. "This is only for a day or two until we sort out some other arrangement."

He sighed and escorted him to his room. The double mattress was large enough for Caden, Deb, and himself on story nights, but wasn't a bed built for sharing with anyone as big as a brute. The guy reeked too. Georges called it garlic, which Henri had a fondness for; plus, he was way too massive. One roll over and Teddy would be done for.

"I sleep on box." He waved a pasty hand at a row of boxes, which made a sort of ledge behind his desk. "I sleep worse." He flushed under Teddy's gaze as though he didn't like to talk.

"Yeah, I guess we could put some blankets and cushions on it."

"'K."

Teddy shook his head, annoyed. He was a brute. He should get angry and demand the bed not slink off to the corner. "That's it? There is no way we can make them comfortable. You're so big the boxes will mush under you. How did you ever become a brute?"

He seemed offended. "What you mean?"

"Well, you're not... it's not like you're... well, you're not intimidating."

Henri blushed again, shifting his bulk with nervous twitching. "Dunno, everyone always thought I nasty 'cause I big, muscle-wise, but," he wiped his nose on his sleeve, "but I like things... 'n people, 'n kittens... especially kittens. Not to eat, though, to pet. Dunno."

Teddy frowned and thought about this, picturing his fellow Underlings trying to get him to fight when he wanted to pet kittens. It was a pathetic image.

"Just a sec," he said, going out into the hall to the back storage room.

He dug up a sturdy length of yellow rope and a couple of large hooks his father said people used to store bicycles on their walls and went back. A bicycle sounded amazing, and he so wanted to find one. He placed it first on his wish list he took with him every time they went scrounging.

"Help me screw this into the wall." He dropped a hook in Henri's hand and pointed to where the paint peeled away, revealing the nails and joints underneath. "Right there, into the stud."

Henri gave him a blank expression. "'K"

Teddy suspected shrugs and 'k' took up the vast majority of his vocabulary. He took a cover from his bed and secured a length of cordage to each corner. Then he passed over another anchor and gestured toward the opposite wall. After double- checking his knots, he looped one rope over the hook and tied it, so two corners of the blanket hung suspended from the floor. He did the same to the other end when the brute finished his part.

"Cool," he said, looking quite pleased and yet puzzled. "What's that?"

"It's a bed," Teddy said, hoping the ropes would hold. "You lay on it."

His face crumpled with concerned. He stared at the blanket swinging free above the ground and scanned his bulk. "Don't think will stay up."

He laughed. "Not you. Me. You can take the bed."

The massive brute gawked at the lumpy old mattress. The springs were worn and stuck through the fabric, making sleep a complicated game of where to lie without skewering yourself. It wasn't much of a bed, but it kept a person off the floor.

Henri snuffled, and Teddy realized he was crying. The brute wiped his face with his sleeve. "Your bed, not mine."

He put a hand on Henri's arm. "I don't mind. I'm kinda excited at getting to sleep in my airbed. My Pa says they're called hammocks, but that's a strange word. I think it'll be like sleeping on a cloud."

"What's a cloud?"

"Things floating in the sky. Rain pours out of them."

"Are you back to the weather?" Jolon asked, limping into the room. He took up his usual spot in his chair. "You got a real thing for stormy nights, don't you?"

"What's that?" asked Deb as she came in with Caden in tow.

"It's an airbed," Teddy told them with pride while hoping the knots and hooks held his weight.

"How's that a bed?" Caden inched in behind Jolon's chair and kept an eye in Henri's directions as though he were a danger waiting to burst into violence at any moment.

"Hi, I'm Deb." She stuck out her hand at the brute.

Jolon plucked a magazine from the floor and flipped through, perusing the pictures. "She's the house nuisance."

Henri waved at her, and she hugged him. "You're like my bear."

He stroked her head as if petting a spider's web and he didn't want to break even a strand.

"So, how do you get in?" asked Caden as she ignored Henri's presence.

Good question. Teddy ran a hand down the blanket's edge, pushing on it. The ropes held. He leaned harder, hopeful; his airbed stayed. With a deep breath, he eased into his bed, hoping the blanket wouldn't flip and throw him on the ground. The bed wiggled under him, making him freeze and Caden laughed.

"You should see your face. Your eyes are so wide."

"Ha, ha," Teddy lay back and stretched out. The blanket held him in a cocoon, and the swinging was quite soothing as he relaxed.

"It stayed!" Jolon cheered with surprise.

"Soon you'll rival Pa with your inventive contraptions."

His little sister gave the hammock a push. "Can I take a turn?"

"Maybe tomorrow; don't do that."

"Yeah, Deb, it might collapse in the night, and we'll find a Teddy blob on the floor in the morning," Caden said and held out her hand. "Come on, let's put us both to bed."

"But I want a story."

"Not tonight, kid." She ushered Deb out the door with a wary eye on their new addition.

"Don't warp yourself, Henri, she'll warm up to you," Jolon said.

He stared after them, confusion on his face again. "She's purdy." They exchanged a worried glance.

"Roll it in, buddy, she's seven," Jolon said in an authoritative voice Teddy had never heard before.

"No, the other, the tall one, she's so nice."

"Caden?" he asked.

"Yeah, Caden." The brute sighed and flopped on the bed, and stared up at the grey tiling with a dopy, spacey expression.

"Well, that's... uhh...."

"Unexpected," Jolon finished for him.

They traded a worried glance.

"You tell her," his brother whispered with a side-glance at Henri, but he was oblivious to everything. "Are you kidding? I don't need the bruises."

"Hey, she might be pleased."

Teddy lay in his cocoon, swaying and sleepy. "Doubt it." Jolon slapped his hands on the arms of the chair and stood.

"I think I'll go to bed now too. I don't think my brain can handle any more revelations. It's going to take a whole night of sleep to put my head back together as it is. Night, strange people."

Henri grunted something and Teddy closed his eyes.

Chapter 3

Teddy sat on a plastic bin, munching a couple of stale crackers and surveying the land of clutter, which made up their livelihood.

So, what was a mall? From the descriptions in the magazines he collected, it was a place where lots of people went and bought things. Didn't sound much different than the market. Well, what else was there to do? The city was only about ten miles in circumference. It was not as though he could strike out on his own and conquer the world. This was the world; piles and piles of scrounged merchandise, leftovers from a time long gone. He spit out his last cracker. Sometimes stale was too much to take.

"Ma would kill you for wasting food," Caden said as she and Jolon joined him.

"Pa ready to go yet?" he asked.

His brother snatched the box from him and nibbled on a wafer. "Na, Mr. Mitchum is coming to talk to him about some furniture his wife wants."

"Mitchum? Isn't he the one who owns the greenhouse on Northside?"

"Nah." He stuffed his mouth with food. "That's Norton. Mitchum owns the hen house." His last few words came with a shower of crumbs and Teddy brushed them away.

"Yegh, gross." Caden took a scrap piece of paper from the end table by the bed and started scribbling pictures. "You keep eating every moment, and you'll get too big to fit through the tunnels."

He made a face at her but put the box away. "I'm nervous; makes me hungry."

"Hey, you ever wonder what they feed those chickens?" asked Teddy.

"What'd ya mean?" said Caden.

"Well, there is little food for people let alone chicken, and we're not even mentioning water levels. Do chickens drink water?" asked he and her expression turned mocking.

"No, they absorb moisture from the air through their feathers. Doesn't everything living drink, oh educated one?"

A rush of heat covered Teddy's cheeks. "Must be tired. Get all kinds of nonsense questions rolling through my brain when I'm sleepy."

"I don't ask those questions. Don't want to know the answer."

Whether she was right or not didn't stop him from wondering about everything around him.

"Why are you nervous?" he asked Jolon to alter the conversation.

His brother waved to Henri standing by their father at the front desk. The brute was petting the dogs with Deb. He tripped over a bag of nails and fell; Critter jumped on him and slobbered on his face.

"He's terrifying, he is." He shook his head.

"We are in so much trouble," said Caden.

"Come on, Cad, let's give him a chance," Teddy said.

"Yeah, you do that." She started to work her way down from their perch. "I'm gonna bring Deb back to Ma before our 'visitors' show."

Sighing, he decided he didn't want to stick around either. Instead, he and his brother made their way to the curving staircase behind them. It was half gone, but if they grabbed hold of the railing, they could climb to the platform above. He scrambled up easily, but Jolon found the journey more difficult, and he huffed and puffed while Teddy helped him up.

"Cad is right. You gotta cut down on the food." He fell backward as his brother lurched forward with a wild yelp.

"How about you two stop picking at me about it?" said Jolon, his face flushed and hurt. "I got my insecurities just like you guys. Don't need either of you throwing them in my face."

A wave of guilt brought heat to Teddy's cheeks as he got off the floor. He clapped his brother on the shoulder. "Sorry, Jol."

"I come too? Your father said make scarce." Henri stood on the stairs, smiling at them and nodding.

He beckoned to the brute to join them. What the hell, why not? He dusted his pants before going to the end of the ledge and opened the door to a room about ten by ten feet with a large window with a view of the floor below. The desk, chair, and bookshelf were already there from the previous owners. The shelves overflowed with his books from school and any other scraps of stories he collected. He smuggled in a few things to make the space more personal: blankets, pillows, and a few cushions from dilapidated couches. This was where he went when he needed to be alone during the day.

His brother slid down the wall in a corner, his face sweaty. "Okay, so maybe a few less cookies and a little more running around in circles."

"Good room," the brute said, taking up most of the space. "You like books."

He nodded.

"Like 'em," Jolon cut in, "he lives for them. Knowledge to him is like...."

"Food to you?"

"Ha, ha... I get it, all right? Two-second apology and you're done."

Henri checked him over. "You not so big."

Jolon cocked his eyebrow and scanned him too. "Not compared to you, I guess."

The brute rubbed his broad stomach and laughed. "All muscle."

Teddy chose a book from a pile and started to read. "Yeah, that's something only in Jol's head."

"Wow, you can be sooooo not funny."

"Hey, that's what siblings are for, right? Ow!" he yelped as Jolon whacked him with a book.

"That's what siblings are for too," his brother said, making a face.

He scowled back. "You're not exactly pure water and fresh veggies with the side comments either."

"'K, fine. You lay off the body jokes, and I'll lay off any violent retaliations, fair?"

"Fair," agreed Teddy and went back to his book.

"Where go?"

He glanced up from his story. "What? Oh, That's a vent, I think, or at least, something similar. I never took the cover off 'cause you can never tell what lurks up anywhere," he said as he realized the brute was talking about the opening in the ceiling.

Henri kept staring at the grate as though he expected something to appear. "Why not go up?"

"Like he said, we don't know what's up there," said Jolon in an exasperated voice.

He stared at them both as though they didn't make sense. "So, go up and check, yes?"

"So, go check, no," Teddy threw his book aside as he realized he could not read with Henri around. "You ever scrounge?" The brute shook his head. "No? Well, we're scroungers from childhood and we understand you don't go poking about just because."

"Too dangerous," his brother said.

"Exactly."

Henri sighed, his face sagging with disappointment. "Some day, you go."

Teddy went to the window, his curiosity nagging at him. He couldn't tell if the guy made a statement or asked a question. "Don't push."

"Yeah, too late. Forget it, Ted," Jolon told him as he placed his hands on the windowsill. "Listen to your own advice."

Right, forget. That would be fun to do.

"You two good friends," Henri observed with a wistful expression. "Don't you have any friends, family, or anyone?"

He shook his sad head. "No, none. Just Georges and she okay. Had one friend years ago. Big ruddy buddy, Keme. He nice long time. He disappeared, taken to brute auction. Never saw again. Heard he got picked by clever Upperlord, but nothing else."

"Time to move, gophers. I do believe we're wanted." Jolon tapped his fingers on the glass and waved at Pa below.

He stood by the service desk signalling to them as three men in black suits strode away with their two massive brutes hauling their merchandise behind them.

"Why can't you be like them?" asked his brother, gesturing to the two walls of meat glaring like they could burn through cement with their eyes.

Henri seemed hurt and confused. "I don't?"

"No."

The guy flexed his biceps. "I as big."

"It's not the size, buddy." Jolon turned to Teddy with a silent plea for an explanation.

"Don't listen. You're fine the way you are," he said, sticking his tongue at his brother.

They scrambled down to the warehouse floor and joined their father.

"So this is your brute," said Dorkas, a fellow scrounger. He stepped around a shelf of dishware and plastic bins, his face cracked with sores and scars. The creep poked a finger at Henri and sneered. "Piece of the scum-riddled bottom of the sewer, ain't he?"

Pa gave the guy a tight smile and a couple of credits. "Thank you for the goods, Dorkas. I'm sure I'll be able to find someone who wants them. If you get any more, drop by," he said as he escorted the man out of their warehouse.

A shiver ran up Teddy's back as the creeper left. "Why do you do business with him? He's the worst sort of garbage."

His father scrubbed his hair and sighed. "Yes, he is not the type one trusts, but I like to keep an eye on him. He could cause more trouble otherwise."

"He was lingering about the Adult Quarter yesterday with some toady, greasy character."

His father grasped his stash. "Not surprising. I don't trust him, and he doesn't trust me, but we pretend we do. You don't want to lose track of a man like him."

Two hours later, they arrived at Montgomery Mall once more. Caden stayed behind. Her illness was one, which often overcame Underlings especially those born near the pits on the lower South Side where sludge and noxious fumes flowed. The further south one went the more warped the bodies and minds.

Teddy had been lucky and grew up in the stability of Northside where life was the closest to normal. The warehouse was in North Side as well. Pa's family worked hard to establish their territory and keep them safe.

He leaned his shoulder against the wall beside the room he suspected was an elevator and adjusted his mask.

"Okay, Pa, where do we go from here?"

His father scrunched his eyes and tapped his pant leg as he thought about their next move. "The map says this is level three, and the area is solid rubble in that direction," he said, indicating the glass entrance. "So, either this whole building is buried, which would kill our ambitions, or, if luck pays us a visit, the first two levels are clear." He cast his light in a circle as he turned. "Let's try the elevator first."

"Why?" he asked, straightening. "We have no electricity; we can't use it."

"Yes, but you never know. We might be able to climb down the shaft." Pa took out the crowbars and passed him one. Together they forced the doors open. His father shone a light in, and Teddy gasped.

The tiny room was filled with bodies, corpses of men, women, and children, all trapped and dying centuries ago in a place with nothing, but a few buttons on the wall. He turned away, gagging. This wasn't the first time he found remains, but he still hated it.

Pa let the doors close. "Let's try the next one. This is the best tomb we can give them." He went over to the other exit and pushed the silver bar that opened the door with ease. "Well, come on. Let's explore where this leads."

They came to a clear stairwell, and the only direction was down. Pa trotted on ahead. As they reached the next platform, the stairs turned and continued downward. There was another door on the landing after that. He pushed the bar. This one stuck. He passed Teddy the light and shoved until they could make their way through. They checked the air quality and removed their respirators.

He scratched his head where the band of the mask caused an itch while they made their way into the open. The left was a solid mix of debris and dirt. He did not peer too close in case he discovered more bodies. How the right side of the building managed to come away almost unscathed was more than he could figure out, but it was a lucky break for them.

"Pa, what do you think life was like back before the meteors?"

"Strange and wondrous. Hey, shine your handlight over here."

He turned his lantern in the angle his father wanted. His light glinted off a tall glass window, and he jumped as a bizarre woman stared back. He had gasped before he realized she wasn't moving. He came closer, and his father went through the door. Teddy joined him, keeping a careful eye on the statue-woman. It was creepy, unnatural, and made him tremble. He tried to turn his attention to the rest of the room.

"Look at this place," Pa said, excited. "If even half of this merch is any good, we are in business." He worked through piles of clothing and displays scattered everywhere and reached the main desk in the centre of the room. "Check for anything useful," his father said as he rooted through some drawers.

Teddy pulled out a blue dress filled with holes and stained with things he did not want to identify. Something scurried in some clutter to his left and what he thought was a shirt, moved. Rats, mice, and bugs made their home in whatever they could. "Ah, Pa? I'm not too sure any of this will be any good."

"Hmmm. Check the clothes still hanging. There's little chance anything lives in them. Keep an eye out for ratdogs. Haven't seen any yet, but ya never can tell."

Gingerly, Teddy crept over to the first rack on the wall, a cluttered selection of pants and tops. They were the kind of goods the Upperlords paraded around in and scroungers near the vast crater in West Side supplied. Their leader was a large woman with pox marks and sores all over her skin, which she hid under layers and layers of cloth and jewels. She piled her hair high on her head and always had at least two or three decorations stuck in the coils.

He turned toward his father who was collecting a satchel of jewellery. "This stuff might put us in direct competition with Madame Belle. I'm not sure Henri can stand against her temper."

Pa snickered. "True. Who can say? She might fall for his sweet innocence. Still, you may be right."

"Um, how about we go and check what else is here before we start stockpiling this stuff?"

His father stored his satchel in the side pocket of his stash and brushed off his hands. "Good idea."

They left the store, and he was happy to leave the mannequin behind. The stall next door was filled with broken glass and pieces of dishes. A skeletal hand stuck out from behind one of the displays near the back.

"Let's go back to that one later," Teddy said, backing away. He didn't want to see anymore.

As they searched on, the hall branched off to their left. They paused, and he shone his handlight forward. Mud and debris blocked their way.

"Appears we turn," his father said.

"Hope so. Otherwise this is it."

His father shook his head. "Nah, there must be more. I can feel it." He flashed his light down the other way. "You notice the air?"

Closing his eyelids, Teddy stood still, breathing deep. "It's cool and moves."

"Yep." Excitement danced in his eyes. "It moves... it's a wind...."

Teddy's heart leapt. "Mechanical or, or," the words did not want to come out, "natural?"

His father took hold of his arm. "Who cares? Both send the blood stirring. Imagine, just imagine, Teddy, either something is making the air," he paused, his nose wrinkling as he sniffed, "fresher and moving, or this is real air." His tone dropped to a whisper, as though afraid he would spook the breeze if he spoke too loud. He took out his tester. "All is good. Pure enough to breathe."

Teddy stared at him. Either possibility was overwhelming to think about. These passageways were their life. A shiver went down his back—to get out of Undercity.... He once asked his teacher why they lived underground when the farmers and the greenhouse people talked of clear skies. His teacher told him the story of how they did attempt to re-establish life outside right after the meteor strike. According to him, the entire team of researchers died an agonizing death. Since then, they passed a law keeping everyone inside and no one ever brought up the issue again.

"Pa, we can't..."

He draped an arm around Teddy's shoulder. "Oh, my boy, you're getting worried over nothing. I have no scheme, no real desire in attempting to go outside. I've seen the pictures and stood by the memorial, but we might be able to establish a better life for the Underlings."

"A new city?"

"A new city. A new city where everyone gets to live in homes with the basic necessities without having to grovel and depend on anyone else."

"The Uppers won't like that."

He touched Teddy's nose and winked. "That's why we keep this a secret. That's why we got a brute."

"You don't think Henri will be much use against the Upperlords, do you? I'll agree he is powerful, but he's harmless. I doubt he would hurt a bug, let alone stop the Uppers taking over this place."

"He's a beginning. From this point on, we go slow and careful."

Careful indeed. They would need to creep along in baby steps by his thinking. "Pa, if one hint of this gets around in Upper, they'll descend on us like a dirt slide. They'd lose their workers, their power. They might even need to work for themselves, and that would not go over well at all."

His father didn't respond as they continued. He held his light high to show their path. The wall to the right was solid and covered with the words 'Celporia, Opening soon. A New Way To Be Fashion.'

"There might be merchandise behind the sign," Teddy said, peering close.

"Just a cursory search today," Pa said and kept moving.

In the next window was a large picture with grand splotches of green and gold lights behind a group of people performing what he figured must be music.

Music—a few Uppers owned the few instruments found by the Underlings. They were special people, almost more elite than those who controlled the water, food, and air. However, they had a limited song selection and restricted public performances to a yearly concert. Otherwise, they played at the sole discretion of other Uppers. He shuffled into the store with a touch of reverence. Songs were enticing, haunting; the melodies locked in his head and stayed.

Strange little cases with bizarre pictures all over them filled the rows of bins. It was music, at least, that's what the signs said, but how did one listen to the stuff? He picked one case up and shook it. The contents rattled, so he peeled off the thin plastic covering and opened the case. A round disc lay inside. He popped the object out, examined every facet, and still didn't understand where the music hid.

"Teddy, anything useful?"

He gave a negative sway to his head, dejected. "No. At least, I don't think so." Throwing the disc back in a bin, he sighed. One day he would think of a way to figure out how things worked.

"Hey, wait, I think I struck riches," he said as he caught sight of a display of batteries on his way out. He took down several packs of different sizes and gave some to his father who dumped them in his stash.

"Great stuff. If they are still good, we've got enough here to last for quite a while. Found some candles too, in glass holders with little green balding creatures on them." He picked up a book lying on a pile near the wall. "New reading for you."

"Yeah, lots." He took the novel, a thrill running through him at the thought of a new story. The cover was shiny with a picture of a pale humanoid figure glaring back at him. He turned the hardcover over in his hands before stuffing the book in his pack. "For later," he said, resisting the urge to open the pages.

They moved on, their footsteps making the only sound. This place seemed endless. It was amazing how little damage the area sustained. Sure, a whole bunch of trash lay scattered all over, and many of the glass windows shattered, but the structure seemed to be okay. At least, he didn't detect any cracks or fractures in the brown stucco walls and the fixtures, though dead with a lack of power, still hung from overhead. He tried to picture the place as it was—the lights high above shining bright, people wandering from shop to shop—everything seemed colourful and exciting. Now, it all was empty and broken. At least, he hoped it was empty.

"Pa, how do we know nobody lives here?"

His father stopped and turned, his face cautious. "What do you mean?"

"Well, if our people survived with all the damage our cities suffered, how do we know a similar city of survivors doesn't live here? The place is ideal."

Pursing his lips, his father thought about this. "Good question. We've seen a few bodies, yes, but we haven't seen any signs of anyone living." He waved toward the soiled hall. "If there were survivors, you'd think we'd find footprints and a lack of dirt. Plus, little usable merchandise available to us." He stepped over a clutter of bags spilling out their items and stood in front of the next store. "All this stock, these dishes, the clothes, everything sits here as though waiting for people to return. No, I think if anyone ever lived down here, they are long gone."

Teddy gazed around. His theory made sense, but he still felt uneasy. "I guess."

"Tell you what," Pa said, putting his hand on his hip. "We have gone far enough for today. How about we gather a few things to bring back to your mother and next time we'll take Henri with us just in case."

This did not make Teddy feel much better, but he helped his father pick out some choice clothing for the others. He lifted up a pair of long pants. "If these fit, that would be terrific." He glanced down at his worn brown trousers with the tears in them. "I haven't had anything this good in a couple of years."

His father laughed, and held up a soft green dress with little white flowers. "Your ma will be so beautiful in this."

Teddy caught his father's excitement and found a flowing purple top, more pants, and a few decent tops. "Caden might not appreciate this, but she deserves something new. These trousers should work for Jolon, and we can share the shirts." He dug up a large black and red jacket covered in skulls and bones. "Do you think Henri would fit this? Maybe it will make him appear tougher."

Pa grinned. "It might."

They laughed at the abundance their treasures gave them, but still, Teddy had a nagging sensation that this was all too easy.

His father patted his back. "Come on, son. We can't take too much. Might draw unwanted attention, right?"

He gave a disparaging grimace. "Yeah. Wouldn't want to wander outside of our place."

"No, no, not yet. Our day will come."

Teddy trailed behind his father as he guided them out of the building. Glancing back, he thought he caught a glimmer of something, but it disappeared in seconds, and he hoped it wasn't a ratdog or worse. He clasped his knife just in case and hurried after his father. Their footsteps cascaded through the hall and up the stairs. He peered down the stairwell.

"How far down do you think this goes?"

"Who can say? Might go to another floor, or three or four. We'll find out soon enough."

"Three or four floors? If they are in as good a shape as this one, we might be able to house more people than the whole population of Undercity."

His father frowned. "Let's not get ahead of ourselves. We still need to find a clean source of water, a proper sewage system, and confirm a healthy source of air."

Teddy felt the sombre weight of doubt in the bottom of his stomach. "And we need to find a way to grow plants, don't we? Plus, fix the other staircase, so it's sound enough for everyone to cross."

"There's that, too." Pa agreed. "Yep, this is an extensive project." His voice faded, and Teddy could tell he was mulling over all the details that went into changing their world.

"So, what do I do with this?" Caden asked, holding up the blouse he found for her. She raised an inquisitive eyebrow.

"Wear it?"

"Ha, ha."

Deb twirled around in a new orange and white dress speckled in blue dots. "It's beautiful." She touched the top. "If you don't want this, can I keep it?"

Caden jerked the shirt away. "No, it's too large for you and it's mine. Too bad you didn't find any pencils. Mine are all stubs. Can't draw too much with stubs." She wandered over to a chair and sat, her face pale under her sepia complexion.

"I'll keep a lookout for some next time," he said and turned toward his mother, and she met his gaze.

Ma took him by the arm and led him to his room. "Come, Teddy, let's see how these pants fit you." Henri wasn't around. Pa needed his assistance to secure the secret door.

"I like the bed you made yourself," his mother said, pushing on his airbed. "You sure it won't fall?"

He pulled off his old pants, tossing them on a box in the corner. His shirt covered enough of him to make him less uncomfortable about undressing in front of her. "It's fine, Ma."

"Oh, I'm certain it is. You are a copy of your father, always inventing things," she said with a smile. "You might not be blood, but you are your father's son."

The thought made him happy. "How is she?"

His mother sighed and sat on his bed, tweaking the leg of his trousers. "Caden? The day has been difficult for her."

"Ma, you gotta take her to the doctor. I understand he doesn't help anyone unless they can pay, but there must be a way."

"It's not just paying, Teddy."

He tugged at his pants. "We found all this new junk; we could use some to see him."

"He doesn't treat Underlings no matter how much they offer him." Her voice stuck in her throat. "And he doesn't have to. He doesn't have to. No laws exist to make him and he is the only medical person in the city. No one else possesses the knowledge he does. The profession was a tradition passed down from his ancestors, which they didn't share with anyone else." She threw her hands up, her eyes glistening with tears. "There's nothing we can do except love her and comfort her."

"Not right," said Henri as he appeared, filling the doorway.

"Oh, Henri, yes," Ma said. Weariness hunched her shoulders as she stood. "I know, but some things no amount of muscle can alter."

His open, happy face crumpled and Teddy clasped his shoulder.

"I don't understand either. No one seems bothered by a few slugs thriving off the suffering of others. I think things were different once. At least, that's what the books I've read say. It's possible those are only stories or myths. I don't know. Not important, I guess."

"It matters."

Ma kissed Teddy on his forehead. "Yes, but a good night's sleep will help. The pants are good. Wear them out a little before you venture beyond our walls. Don't want to stir up any attention." Her tired voice cracked as if she wished they didn't play so many games to survive. She patted Henri on his broad shoulder as she left the room, and he swayed his head.

"Teddy?"

He sat down in the hammock and let it swing. "Yeah?"

"We can fix?"

As Teddy laced his fingers behind his head, he contemplated the giant who stood wringing his hands. The jacket fit him and made him seem a little tougher, but too much kindness and emotion shone from him. His eyes danced as though searching his brain for a thought, a plan. "We'll try."

"We'll try what?" Jolon asked, sauntering in. He didn't carry any bugs or food and his new clothes almost made him appear as though he belonged up top despite his slight limp.

Henri dumped himself on the bed. "To fix this."

He made a face. "To fix what?"

"Our situation," Teddy said, knowing he was vague, but not certain how to share the thoughts crowding his brain. "Where are the others?"

His brother plopped in his chair. "Deb is attempting to read Caden a story. She is enduring it because she can rest and the parents are in the warehouse dealing with a visit from the Mercury brothers. Someone wants to purchase a wedding dress and four matching bridesmaids' dresses and they must get them now."

Teddy snorted. "Luck with that."

"Yeah, finding a matching anything these days is almost impossible, but it's one of the greenhouse baron's daughters marrying one of the water barons. She's sixteen, and he's something like fifty. He was the guy who turned up last week complaining he shouldn't have to go through any middle people; he should be able to purchase things directly from us. Now Ma and Pa need to soothe ruffled feathers and assure Mercury Brothers Inc. They have no intention of going against convention."

Frowning, Teddy sat up. "We should go help."

"I can fix."

"Na, they want to appeal to them on a more passive level. Any show of strength may cause them to think we're hiding something," Jolon said.

Henri bounded to his feet, pacing. "Why hire brute if I can't brute?" He jabbed at his chest. "I fix."

For a moment, he almost believed him except his eyes were glistening. "We don't need impulsive actions; we need cool, calm planning."

"Don't get wired, big guy." Jolon patted the brute's leg. "You'll get your chance. Don't want to tip our hand too fast."

Teddy laughed. "You look like a cheap gambler," he said as his brother put his feet up. "You were sneaking off to the games at Under Smith's again?"

He spread his hands and tried to appear innocent. "Speaking of gambling, you and Pa find anything interesting aside from clothes today?"

"Dead bodies, skeletons. That sort of debris."

Jolon's eyes were wide, and he moved to the edge of his seat. "Honest?" He sat back, blinking. "Bet you were scared shitless."

"Was not."

His brother laughed. "Yeah, bet you tossed your cookies."

"Did not," he snapped though he could feel his face flushing. "Okay, let's go and see how you do."

"Yes."

The two of them stared at Henri, surprised by the brute's word.

"What do you mean? Yes, what?" Teddy asked.

"Yes, go. Explore. We know here. Nothing for likes of us. Might be something there. Don't you want find out?"

"We, we can't," Jolon insisted, his voice shaking. "Pa never lets us go into the tunnels without him, and Ma will skin us and feed us to the dogs."

Henri stared at them, expectant and serious, his jaw clenched, but his eyes innocent and hopeful.

"So what do you think, shiny knight syndrome or boredom?" Jolon asked.

"Either that or love at first sight, but I think that's a plot device to save time."

His brother cocked an eyebrow. "Oh, you need new books to read, don't you? Plot device, okay, but we can't go exploring alone. Pa says we need to be careful."

"Yeah, but a little more research shouldn't hurt much," Teddy decided with a shrug.

Jolon choked. "You're kidding."

He shook his head. "Come on, Jol. It's time to show me just how brave you are."

"Funny. You know I don't own a brave bone in my body."

"Well, maybe it's time we found one." Teddy hopped to his feet and took Henri's hand. "Okay. Let's do this."

The brute took on a toothy expression. "K."

Chapter 4

O nce they were certain everyone slept, Henri helped them uncover the door, and they entered the tunnels. They continued in silence for a while, inching their way through the passages. The darkness seemed deeper without their father's presence. Their footsteps boomed as they reverberated all around. It was as though all the ghosts of the past lingered behind them in a drawn-out procession to their doom.

"You are joking," said Jolon when they got to the lower level of the mall.

"This not so bad," Henri said, striding behind them with his light held high over their heads.

"It's dark. I hate dark. I lived in dark for too long," his brother went on, his voice warbling.

"We all have," Teddy said, feeling uneasy too. "I understand, Jol, but things are not too horrible down here or up here. I'm not sure. We went down the stairs, but we went up and up before we got here. Those passages back there go through so much rubble nothing makes much sense even with the map. This place was a lucky find. I don't like the dark either, but here we are. We can't escape the darkness. We can't do anything. At least, that's what they say. That's what they all say. Could be true or we're all wishing for a different destiny. This is all ridiculous. We're here because our ancestors wanted to save themselves. Well, if this is saving themselves, maybe this wasn't the right choice. I don't know."

"Ted."

"Hey, what kind of life is this? We only live by the whim of people who only want to parade around acting all wonderful."

"Teddy, calm yourself."

"And they're not. They're not. They are people like us. They possess as much value as anyone else. This is ridiculous. In fact, they are less because they can't see other people are as good as them." He jerked around as Henri yanked his arm.

"Done?"

Panting, he shook himself, all the tension in his body dispersing at once in a ranting stream of words. "D... d... done," he gasped trying to regain his composure. "Sorry. Don't know why I did that."

"'Cause you're weird," Jolon said, clapping him on the back. "But we all are, so relax. Besides, you made me feel better."

"That's good, I guess."

"Yeah, after your freak out, I realized I didn't want to seem like a baby like you."

"Funny." He shook himself again and nudged his brother's shoulder. "Come on."

"Shouldn't we explore these a little more?" Jolon asked while they passed the stores.

"Nah, Pa and I searched these before," he said as he hurried to keep up with their brute. "Besides, I think Henri's on a mission. Henri? What do you think you'll find? Can we slow down a bit? You might not be aware of this, but our legs are not as long as yours."

"Yeah," Jolon added with a hand to his side. "And this exercise thing is a heap of garbage. No, it's a mountain of garbage mixed with toxic waste, cooked in a volcanic river, and thrown up by the belly of the earth."

"Imaginative. Finished?" Teddy asked, with a raised eyebrow.

"Yes, in fact, finished, finished. I should be guarding the door back at safety central. And thank you. I've been working on my imagination. You can't be the only one making up stuff." He stopped and bent over, puffing. "What are you seeking, Henri? Something good, I hope 'cause I ain't going through this for anything less than something good."

"A way out," the brute admitted, pacing. "This can't be all. Stories, tales people tell. Can't read, but listen and must be more—for all. Nice place where all okay."

Teddy turned to Jolon, dubious.

His brother shrugged. "That's something good."

"Can't get much better."

They grinned and went forward again, searching for even one clue to a real life. Most of the stores they passed carried clothes. He guessed their ancestors had an obsession with garments and shoes, which they found in abundance. Everything seemed surreal. The plastic people didn't bother him now though he still didn't like the ones with heads—too life-like. Soon, they reached what seemed to be the end and another set of glass doors. Something glowed beyond them. They all stopped and stared.

Teddy's heart raced.

"You think?" Jolon asked, nudging him.

"Seems too easy."

"Too easy? The last ones to go out burned alive. I don't call that easy."

"No, I mean the glow, if that's outside, shouldn't it be harder to get at than stepping through a door?"

"Don't care," Henri said and strode forward.

"Wait," he shouted, but the brute didn't listen. The door pushed debris to the side as he shoved it open. Teddy rushed to put on his mask but was too late. The stale air hit him hard. He tried to hold his breath while he fumbled for his respirator. His sight dimmed, and he began to see stars. He went under, his mask in hand.

When he opened his eyes, Henri's huge face bobbed before him, his bulbous nose inches from his.

"K? K? Ted? Teddy. I sorry. I not think. Oh, wake up." He shoved the mask on Teddy's face.

He swatted at the brute's hand. "Don't shake. I'm okay. Stop."

Henri pulled off the oxygen mask. "What?"

"I said stop." He coughed and sat up, taking a breath or two from his tank. "How's Jol?"

"Alive," his brother moaned, not far from him. "The hulking pack of muscle shook the death right out of me."

"Sorry, sorry," Henri said over and over. "Didn't mean to. Didn't think."

"Okay, all is good," said Teddy, his head throbbing a fraction. "Slow down, 'k? Sometimes when you open a sealed area, you get hit with bad air. Kinda like a punch to the jaw."

"Well, I was right," said Jolon, rubbing his temples.

"'Bout what?"

"This was too easy."

Teddy laughed. Still a little wobbly and light-headed, he rose to his feet. He took another shot of oxygen. The door was still open; the air must have stabilized. He gazed at Henri. "How come you didn't go under?"

He gave a timid grin and held up his mask. "Bigger person, more air in me. Had time. Sorry."

"Always thought you were somewhat of an airhead," Jolon muttered but patted Henri's arm. "So, do we go on, or go home? It's gotta be getting late by now, and they'll discover we're gone if we're not at breakfast." His stomach grumbled, revealing his real concerns.

Teddy took a crisp biscuit from his supplies. "Here, nibble this."

"Oh, perfect, cookie power. Got another?"

He grinned and gave his brother one more. "Okay, by my figuring, we have been down here for about three hours... two hours to get here and another hour searching around. So, we can afford another hour before heading back in time to get a moment's sleep before Ma comes for us. Do we go or do we come back tomorrow night?"

Henri shifted from foot to foot and pulled at his trousers.

"Do you gotta go?" Jolon asked.

The brute blushed. "Yes."

"Uh, huh," said his brother and stood. "So do I. I'm finding a corner before continuing. Saves any embarrassment in case of flight."

Teddy went and located a pillar off to the side to relieve himself. Between the debris and decay, he figured a little urine wouldn't cause much more work to clean up if Underlings came to live here. As he did up his pants, he paused, certain he heard movement in the store nearby. He told himself it was something small, but the nagging voice inside his head didn't agree. The sound was too human. Keeping his eyes glued on the eerie room, he backed his way to the others.

"Ummm, walking works better when you face where you're going," Jolon said, touching his back.

"I heard something," he admitted, and they all peered in the direction he had come. The three of them waited, staring.

"It was a rat," Jolon whispered.

"Sure," Teddy whispered back.

"Yes, rat," agreed Henri.

"Wait. Rat, rat or ratdog?" asked his brother, his voice panicked. He nudged Henri. "You're the brute; you check."

"Don't like rats or ratdogs." "Maybe something else?"

He scowled. "That helps. Let's go the other way."

"And if we're followed?"

Teddy jerked his thumb toward Henri. "He can deal with it."

Doubtful, Jolon glanced his way and Henri attempted to appear menacing.

"Let's go." He sighed and went forward.

They entered a walkway almost identical to the one they travelled through to the mall the first time. The walls were glass in the past; they could tell by the frames and shards scattered about. Now, they were blocks of mud and rubble. They were not outside, but the light still glowed at the end of the tunnel. Moving together, they approached the next set of doors while keeping an eye behind them in case the noise was more than a rat. Their feet crunched on shards of glass, but no other sound pursued them.

"Masks on," Teddy said, not wanting a repeat of the last time, but he didn't need to worry. Jolon had his on already, and Henri fished his out too. For a moment, Teddy wondered if this was the best idea. What if they discovered nothing? What if they did end up outside and the sun fried them alive? They would be dust their parents would never find. Fatigue was messing with his head—fatigue and fear—that was it. He was fine. They were okay. He took a deep breath and tilted his head toward Henri, who picked up a piece of metal and smashed the glass.

Teddy threw his arm up, protecting his face. He glared at the brute who donned a sheepish grin. "You've wanted to do that for a while?" he asked, his words muffled by his mask.

"Break fun."

Jolon pushed on the bar across the frame, and the door swung open, scraping on the shards spread over the floor. "Fun, yeah. Unnecessary, definitely."

Sick of wondering if it was safe, Teddy went in. If he fried, he fried. His boots crunched on the glass as it ground into the tile.

"What's the glow?" asked Jolon, joining him.

"Couldn't say. Kinda like the same glow in Uppercity, but that's during the day. It can't be day yet. Might be dawn?"

"What's that?" Teddy asked.

"Don't know. Heard a drunken Upperlord talking about it. He said dawn was the glimmer of the morning coming, the dawn of the day. Sounded magical."

"Sounds mushy."

"He was drunk."

"Yeah, they always are."

The area was similar to the last section with a lineup of stores, which appeared to carry the same kind of content as the last one except for one glowing difference, which made them step forward and stare upward. Glass in the roof. Rows of panels shimmering with what Teddy could only decide was the morning light. Shocked at the sight, he took off his mask, forgetting to analyze the quality of the air. It barely registered they could breathe.

"Wow," Teddy said, gasping.

They glanced at each other and started laughing.

"Wahhhoo," shouted Jolon. "That's more beautiful than Uppercity."

He was right. The multitude of windows were free of debris, unbroken, and secure-looking. The glow emanating from them grew until Teddy had no need of his lamp.

"We live here," Henri said, his face tear stained with joy.

"Perhaps," he said with a lengthy sigh as reality settled in. "It might be possible. I mean, yes, we have light, but what about water and soil? What about food or power and consistent air? We don't even know if the structure is safe. There's a lot more to go through than one night is going to show us."

"You sound like Pa," Jolon said.

"So? He only wants the best for us. He wouldn't bring us to this place unless he answered all those questions and a few more I'm too exhausted to think of."

His brother held his hands up. "Hey, I wasn't saying it was a bad thing."

"We should go now," he said, though he didn't want to leave the rising sun. "We've got a ways to go to get back and no more time to explore further."

Henri continued to stare at the sunrise. Teddy tugged his arm.

"Come on, before they find out we are missing. We're cutting things close as it is. All is good. We'll come back. We're changing the world, remember?" He smiled at him, and the brute grinned back, nodding.

"All right, adventurers, let's get out of here. I need my bed," Jolon said, yawning.

The future seemed exciting for once, and this gave them the energy to return home. On the way, they discussed the incredible possibilities their discovery presented. However, once Teddy slipped back into his bed, he was asleep in seconds. Only a moment went by before someone was shaking him. He brushed away the hands touching him.

"Go away."

"Teddy," his mother scolded. "Do not talk to me that way, sleepy or not. What's the matter with you? You're one of the first awake. You sick?" She touched his forehead, and he tried to wake up.

"No, nope. I'm fine. Just stayed up too late..."

"Doing what, writing?" she asked with a disapproving shake of her head.

"Umm, yep, uh-huh, writing. I couldn't sleep so I got up and got inspired. Didn't fall asleep until a second ago."

She frowned with a suspicious glint in her eyes as she brushed strands of hair from his face. "Well, that explains you, but what explains Jolon and," she snapped her fingers at Henri, snoring with vigour under the blankets, oblivious to everything, "I don't know him well enough to know his sleeping patterns, but he does seem to be asleep."

"Jolon is Jolon," Teddy answered. "He's always, well, Jolon."

"Hmmm." She shook her head. "Yes, that pretty much sums him up. Well, your father hopes to get an early start scrounging today, so you better rise, child. I'll get breakfast going while you give yourself a cleaning. It's your turn to bathe first, but hurry, mind you. Deb is wearing more muck on her than those dirt pies she's always trying to make.

Plus, Caden needs a good wash. It'll refresh her and make her feel a little better."

"How's she doing this morning?" he asked, swinging himself out of his hammock.

"Stronger, I think. The coughing isn't so bad, and she is less pale. You can sit with her for a while and tell her a story. She'd like that."

He nodded and plucked a fresh shirt from his pile. She tossed him a towel as she left.

"Don't use all the soap. We are almost out."

Teddy stubbed his toe on the bed and yelped, but Henri only snored and rolled over. He put his towel around his neck and headed to the little room off the main space.

It was a bathroom from days gone by, but the water did not come from a tap to fill the tub. Instead, it dribbled in from a hose protruding through a hole in the wall, which led to a large metal container, which sat over a fire barrel in the kitchen. It functioned well except the system connected to an offshoot from a main pipe supplied by the Uppers. The valve was at their end, which meant they regulated when Underlings would get their water and how much. Pa rigged the bathtub, so the drain went to a filter system he had devised to make the water usable for longer. Still, he was restricted to a hand's span of steamy water to bathe in.

To go first was a treat because the water was clean, but as each person washed up, they added a couple of inches to reheat the tub, so the last one got a full soak. It was a good system, a luxury most people did not possess. Most Underlings owned a drifting, pungent scent similar to rotting rats in a pile of crap, which arrived well before they appeared.

After he had washed, he dried off with a ratty towel decorated with shells and got dressed, wrapping his privates in a cloth he secured around his waist to make his pants more comfortable. Once, he managed to scrounge a wearable pair of briefs, but they wore out a while ago. Still, he never enjoyed the feeling of coarse trousers against the more sensitive parts of his skin. Rubbing his head, he bumped into Deb as he left the room. She grinned at him and held up a fragment of blobby yellow plastic with painted on eyes.

"Ducky and I are going swimming," she said, slipping on the strange goggles Teddy had found for her on one of his scrounges. They seemed to be a useless item in their world, but she loved to wear them under water.

"Wait for Ma before you go in," he told her. "She needs to warm up the water first."

She saluted him. "Yes, sir, I shall secure the area before the general gets here." She started to sing, as loud as her lungs would let her, an odd tune their father had learned from his father. "I got the music in me, I got the music in me, I got the muuuusic in meeeee."

Teddy laughed and thought of all those discs of 'music' he discovered, wondering if her song was on one of them and how a person got to listen. Somehow he doubted she was singing it right.

"Lovely, sweetheart," his mother said as she passed him. "Breakfast is ready. Be sweet and bring some to Caden."

Yawning, he cleared the sleep from his eyes. The bath refreshed him a little, but he was still so exhausted. He snagged a plate, put several pancakes with jam on it, and proceeded to Caden's room as he munched his food.

She sat up in her bed, which took up most of the room. Deb decorated it with everything bright and colourful despite her objections. Bits of cloth of every colour stuck to the wall with pins and streamers dangled from the ceiling.

"Well, you're missing all the fun," Teddy told her as he put the plate on her blanket. "Fuel up. Ma will torture me if you don't. This new?" he asked, glancing at the portrait of Pa displayed with all the other sketches on the wall.

Caden made a face but plucked a potatocake roll. "Yeah. Did it yesterday. What fun?"

"Oh, nothing much. We're just working on a plan; that's all." She licked jam off her lip and arched her eyebrows.

"Who?"

He swallowed and snatched another cake. "Me, Jol, and Henri. It's a surprise for you, and we'll show you once you're better, so rest and get well so you can join us."

"Is that a pep talk? 'Cause it sucks. Why Henri? He's just a brute, a stranger."

Teddy licked his fingers. "Yeah, but he's pretty good. I mean, yeah, he's all soft inside; he cares."

"We don't need a caring brute. They're not supposed to possess feelings or anything human. He's an enormous, overstuffed kitty with no claws. What good is he if we need to protect our home?"

She started coughing, and he gave her a tumbler of water.

"Don't think of those problems. Doesn't do you any good; won't help."

His sister dragged up her blanket and gave him a glare that was more hurt than annoyed. "What should I do, talk about bunnies and flowers as though I know what they are? I'm not you, Teddy. I can't read books and make them come alive in my head. I haven't got the imagination."

"I'll make them live for you," he said, though he wasn't sure what he meant. It seemed to be the best answer he could give. "I'll read to you, I'll sketch them with you, I'll dig holes in this wretched world until I find utopia for you." He grasped her hand and stroked it. "Get better 'cause you're family, and I'm keeping my family. I'll not lose any one of them."

Caden stared at him for a second before she chuckled. "Jeepers, you're a dose of drama, aren't you? Next thing you know you'll be as mushy as our brute." She snatched a slip of paper by her desk and showed it to him. "That was on my pillow this morning when I woke up. Little creepy to think he was in here when I was sleeping, but it was kinda, and I do mean kinda, sweet."

It was a card with balloons floating in a blue sky and the words 'Get Well' over the cream paper. Henri's signature was scrawled in childish letters across the bottom. He must have found it when they were in the mall.

"Sweet," he said with a grin.

She tossed the card aside. "Guess so, but don't ever think I want more of this. In fact, you tell him I'm not in any way interested in his kindnesses. They freak me out."

"If you want me to," he said as he went to get up. The fatigue of his night out was beginning to weigh on him. He ached to snag a little more sleep before his father came looking for him.

Caden grasped his arm as he went to leave. "Well, tell him not to be too mushy."

He laughed. "Yeah, I know; no bunnies."

"What about bunnies?" Deb chirped as she bounced in the room looking fresh and sweet in her new little dress. "They sound cute. What are bunnies?"

"They're the monsters living under the bed and nip at your toes when you won't lie still at night," Caden told her and Teddy hugged her as she squealed in terror.

"Don't pay attention to her, Deb. Bunnies are adorable little creatures with long ears and fuzzy tails."

"Pa's looking for you," Deb said and stuck her tongue out at Caden. "He says you are to meet him in the tank section by the tunnel door."

He stifled a yawn and left them with a wave. So much for catching a little more rest. Still, they would be going back again, which meant exploring the sunshine area in full daylight. Full daylight with all those sky windows, the prospects fired up his spirit, and he quickened his pace.

"How can you be so hyper?" asked a disheveled Jolon as he sat at the table playing with a pancake.

"Pa's going back in the tunnels," he replied as he slung his stash on his back. His oxygen tank needed recharging, and Pa would question him on that. He guessed he could say he didn't recharge it from the other day.

His brother shook his head as he slathered a heavy dose of jam on his potatocake. "Nah, he's not."

Teddy stopped in his tracks. "What do you mean? Ma said he wanted to spend most of the day there."

"Change of plans. 'Parently, Mrs. Fish was here this morning going on about another cave-in, which took out a large part of the Nest, so we're to get whatever cruddy supplies the Uppers don't want and bring them to the survivors."

"The Nest, huh? That's going to be interesting."

"Yeah, what will the Uppers do for cheap entertainment now?"

The cynicism in his brother's voice was understandable, so Teddy ignored it. He had his own disappointments and issues to sort out. True, his goal was to save the rest of Undercity, but now he had to spend the day delivering mothy blankets and loads of potatocakes.

"Jolon, take your bath," Ma ordered, bustling about mixing potato flour and water. "You stink like an old shoe."

"The orphans won't mind, Ma," he said as he stood and licked his fingertips clean. "In fact, the odour might help them be more comfortable."

She thrust her spatula at him. "Wash yourself."

Teddy laughed until she turned her utensil in his direction. "You get to your father. There is much to do and few who are willing to assist, so go."

He turned to escape, but she stopped him with a fling of her spoon, which almost covered him in potato batter. "And get the lump out of bed too. We need all hands today, strong ones."

"How true, how true," Mrs. Fish said as she entered their home.

A stringy lady with little muscle and warm, tawny skin, she had lots of head and mahogany hair. It was an odd picture that left him wondering how her neck could support so much, but she was kind despite how much she liked to talk. She swept her floor-length cloak, with its fading red flowers, around her.

"It is a horrible tragedy. I don't know what we'll do. The elder Underlings are talking of organizing their own government again to address such events. They plan on sending a delegation to meet with the council of Upperlords to ask for some aid and extra water. Doubt they will help. They seem to be determined to exterminate the Underlings, but they'd be in a stew, wouldn't they? Who would do their work for them? They'd need to get dirty and dig for themselves."

Taking up a spatula, she set about turning potatocakes with impressive efficiency. "A few of the other ladies are gathering some rat goop to take as well, but we're short on bandages."

Ma jabbed her spoon at him. "He and his brother can get that together if he ever gets over his wonderful imitation of a statue and gets on with things."

Teddy got the hint and left to get Henri. His mother was one of the kindest, happiest people he ever met, but when serious work needed to be done, she became stern and efficient.

"Hey, Hen, we need you," he said and kicked the bed. The brute grunted and continued to snore. He kicked harder. "Heeennnnrriiiii, wake up, up, up," he shouted. "My Ma is on her way armed with a spoon, and her skirt's in a knot, so we've got to get going."

"Huh, uhhnm?" he said, yawning with a smile on his face as though he was leaving a good dream.

"Come on; we've got to get moving. There's been a cave-in and they need assistance."

That got him started. He bolted upright, still clothed from last night's adventure, and almost knocked Teddy over as he rushed to get out the room.

"Hey, wait up," he called, scrambling after him. "You need breakfast first."

Ma stepped in front of Henri and stuck her spoon under his large nose. "Eat; help after." She tapped her utensil on a fresh plate of potatocakes. "Devour those, and then you two take these containers of food to the wagon. Pa is filling it with blankets and other supplies, and we'll leave as soon as we can."

Jolon ventured out of the bathroom somewhat cleaner than he was before. "Done, Ma. Water's still warm."

She flicked her spoon and showered the floor in remnants of potato. Her wild hair floated about her with a life of its own. "Later. You and Teddy cut up those rags in the bin by the stores of odd statues."

"Ma, you told me to take the potatocakes to the...."

"Just do it," she said, rushing back to her stove.

"But I can't do two things at once," he protested, and she started to cry.

"Just, oh, I don't know, my sweet. It's all so..."

Mrs. Fish put an arm around her. "All right, dear, everything's all right. Teddy isn't trying to cause trouble. He'll do the bandages with Jolon; the big guy can move the bins into the cart. All is well. Let's you and I do the cooking."

His mother nodded, and the boys escaped.

"Wow, this must be a bad one," Jolon said as they entered the warehouse.

Mrs. Fish's husband was stacking supplies in the wagon with Pa. His two sons were with them, taking things from the highest shelves with their long arms. They all had Mrs. Fish character traits—quite tall and strong with sizeable heads while Mr. Fish was stockier with broad shoulders, black hair, bronze skin, and a long beard. Teddy waved at them as he set to work cutting up the cloth with old scissors. He always liked them. They were funny and generous and helped him out a few times when he had been on his own.

"I've never seen Ma in such a state," Jolon added as he grasped some scissors.

"I think she's worn out from existing like this."

"We all are. That's the good part of what we've found. Might mean freedom, right?"

Teddy bobbed his head in agreement. He hoped so, but he was scared. There was still tremendous risk in separating from the Upper-lords and their horde of brutes.

"I suppose."

"You suppose? Did you see that place or were we dreaming? It was stunning, and we didn't get through the whole area."

Teddy snipped and rolled, creating a large pile of multi-coloured bandages. "There's still so much to explore, though, and." His voice went soft as he leaned close. "And we don't even know how safe the place is yet."

His brother made a face. "Safe? Look what we're doing; we're making bandages to try and help a pit load of people injured in a cave-in. There's no doctor, no nurses, no emergency people to pitch in, just us their neighbours. That's it. I don't think life can get worse."

"All right, boys, that'll have to do for now. Mrs. Fish is going to round up a couple of the younger kids to help, so you two can assist with the digging," their mother said as she came up behind them. "Take what you can and let's get going."

They packed the cart with lanterns, blankets, food, and shovels, and dragged the worn wagon after their family as they left for the East Side. The wheels wobbled and creaked in protest of its load as they crossed the bridge. It took a while to get to their destination. Teddy rubbed his eyes as he went, wishing for an hour's more sleep, but he started to see the toll the new cave-in had taken on Undercity and he felt ashamed.

People he knew, people he grew up with huddled in the gloom, crying and moaning. Rubble, broken beams, and broken people—the devastation was frightening. Cement dust filled the air and made breathing difficult.

Coughing, Teddy flicked on another lantern.

"Oh, hell," Jolon said, gazing about. "This is going to be fun. Little light, bad air, and it's hot. Jeeze, it's hot."

They halted at a carved out hollow where members of their mother's emergency committee were putting together an aid station. Several bodies lay in a corner under dirty blankets, and a lineup of people bloodied and wounded, waited for assistance.

"Come on, boys," Pa said; his face twisted grim as they finished unloading the cart. "It's shovelling time."

Jolon swung a shovel to his shoulder. "Eh, not much left to salvage, is there? I hate to be pessimistic, and this might sound bad, but what's the point?"

"Yeah, well, the point is there may still be people alive in pockets."

"In pockets. Yes, in pockets of what? This whole stinking city is the back pocket in the pants of the devil. And now, he's taken a shit."

"And we get to wipe the crap up," Teddy agreed and put his shovel to work.

Chapter 5

After several hours of digging through broken cement and crumbled drywall, Teddy began to doubt they would find anyone else alive.

Dust clogged his throat and he stopped for a moment, propping himself with his shovel as he coughed.

"Here," his father said and passed him a bottle of water.

He took a long sip and then wiped his mouth with the back of his sleeve. "What do you think, Pa? Do we keep searching?" he asked as he passed the bottle back. He gestured toward the mess of dangling beams, fallen wires, and collapsing walls blocking the passage in front of them. "I don't think that ceiling is going to last much longer."

"Or the floor for that matter," Pa said, his brows drawn together with concern.

"Why are you people even bothering?" Dorkas asked as he came up behind them.

While Teddy and his father were covered in muck and sweat, the Undercity creeper was suspiciously clean despite carrying a shovel.

"Didn't know you were here helping, Dorkas," Pa said in a tolerant tone. "Good. The more hands the better."

"Stow the sarcasm, Peterson, I..."

"Look," Pa said, cutting the creeper off with a wave of his hand. He pointed his handlight through the web of rubble. "There, I think there's movement."

Teddy turned his own light to where his father was pointing, squinting to find whatever Pa had seen. Far ahead in the dark, something moved.

"I think it's an arm," he said and crept closer to get a better look.

"Careful," Pa said as he moved a busted pipe aside. "This whole section could go at any moment."

"You people are cracked if you are going to go out there," Dorkas said, backing away.

"Scared, Dorkas?" Pa asked over his shoulder as he slipped under a beam. "Don't worry; you don't have to come."

"Scared? No," the creeper said with a scoffing laugh. "But I ain't foolish enough to risk the ground crumbling under me for a shadow."

"It's not a shadow, listen," Teddy said as he caught the faint call of a voice.

They held still, waiting in the silence for confirmation of help. A low groan and murmur echoed off the stone and cinder blocks, drifting toward them in a barely audible, but definitely living whisper.

"Yep, that's someone," Pa said and began to move rubble aside in a hurry. "Come on, Dorkas, give a hand."

The creeper hesitated, glaring at everyone and everything. Finally, he wiped his nose on the back of his arm and took hold of the wooden beam Pa was trying to shift.

"This ain't gonna move much," Dorkas grunted as they strained against the weight.

Teddy climbed in beside his father and helped as best as he could, but the three of them were barely able to shift the beam more than a foot.

Huffing, Teddy stepped back and put his hands to his knees as they took a moment to rest. Somewhere beyond their barrier more rubble shifted.

"This is too dangerous," Dorkas said, backing away. "I ain't risking my life for any Underling."

"You're an Underling, Dorkas," Pa said, trying to find a way through. "Just like everyone else down here."

"I think I can get through, Pa. I'm smaller than you," Teddy said as he peered through the maze of beams and pipes.

His father took a step back, his hands on his hips and sweat trickling down the side of his face. "I don't know, Ted. This area could go at any moment."

"Which means there's no time to waste," Teddy said and began to climb through the mess.

"Be careful," his father said, holding his lantern high to light the way.

Teddy twisted and wriggled his way around broken vents, dangling wires, and splintered lumber. Dust hampered his breathing while bits of cement and other pieces of debris cut into his hands and knees. The stifling heat sent droplets of perspiration down his forehead and into his eyes. He strained his ears for any sounds of life.

"Anything? Teddy?" his father called. "Ted, answer me, please."

"Yeah," Teddy said and coughed. "Yeah," he said louder. "I think there's room further ahead, but I need more light."

"Coming."

"No, Pa, wait," Teddy said, but was too late as he heard his father working his way toward him.

Unable to think of a way to stop his father, Teddy kept moving forward. His shoulders and back ached from twisting around all the obstacles hampering his way. At the moment when he thought he couldn't get any farther, he pushed aside a slab of wallboard and crawled out into an open area.

He shook dirt and dust from his hair and sat in the low light for a moment to catch his breath.

"You all right?" Pa asked as he appeared with two handlights in one hand. His face was filthy with sweat and filth. He crawled in beside Teddy, his chest heaving from laboured breathing.

"Yeah," Teddy said and wiped his forehead with the back of his sleeve. He took one of the lights from his father. "That was a tight squeeze. I'm surprised you were able to get through."

His father chuckled and rubbed his shoulder. "Wasn't easy. I'm not as limber as I used to be. What was that?"

They both fell silent and turned as they heard a scratching sound not far from where they sat. Teddy swept his light over the area. A small shape huddled by a broken piece of furniture about twenty feet from them.

"I see someone," he said and crept forward. The floor beneath him began to creak and groan the further along he moved. He slid down onto his stomach, spreading out his weight. Another foot further, the ground dropped away and a wide, black hole divided him and the figure on the other side.

"Teddy, get back," his father said. "It's too unstable."

"It's a child, Pa," he replied as he pointed his beam on the person across the way.

The little Underling had to be no more than five or six, and was curled up in a ball, rocking back and forth. Long strands of tangled, dirty hair covered the child's face.

"Hey," Teddy called in a gentle voice. "I'm gonna get you out of here, okay?"

The child didn't respond.

"You have to let me know if you're okay. Are you hurt? Can you move?"

Still, the child just rocked and whimpered.

"Pa, we need something to lay across the hole, so I can crawl over," Teddy said, glancing back toward his father.

After a moment's searching, Pa scrounged up three boards, each about twelve feet long and four inches wide, and pushed them, one by one, over to Teddy.

"I'm not so certain this is a good idea, Ted. Maybe I should do this. Anything happens to you and your mother will never forgive me."

As Teddy slid each board across the opening, the edge of the floor crumbled a little more. "You're too heavy. I'll be all right. Got something to tie these together with? I don't want to have them spread apart right in the middle of crossing."

Pa yanked down a long dangling piece of wire coated in white plastic from the ceiling and tossed it over to him. Teddy looped it around the boards and twisted the ends around each other until the cable held the wood tight together. The makeshift crossing did not appear stable at all, but there was no other way across.

"Okay, I'm going over," Teddy said and took a deep breath. He placed his handlight on the ground so that the beam illuminated the makeshift bridge and the other side of the room.

"Wait a moment, Teddy," his father said and passed him another long piece of wire. "Tie this around your waist. I have enough here for you to get across. That way if you go down, I have some way of getting you back."

"Right. Good idea." Teddy threaded the wire through the loops of his pants and knotted the cable tight.

As his father fed him the wire, Teddy crawled across the boards. His makeshift bridge bowed slightly in the middle from his weight, making him freeze for a moment, as he feared the whole thing would collapse. Without anything to secure the ends to the floor, the planks wobbled and shook. He kept his breath long and slow, concentrating on reaching the other side. By the time he touched the other side, his whole body vibrated with tension.

"Made it," he said and lay down by the hole to recover.

"Good job," Pa said from the other side, his face ghostly in the dim light. "How's the child?"

Teddy sat up and crawled over to the little Underling, who refused to unwind from the foetal position.

"Hey," Teddy said, keeping his voice low. "I'm going to get you out of here, okay?"

The Underling jerked and whimpered louder as Teddy touched the kid's shoulder.

Bits of plaster and wallboard crumbled down around them. Teddy ducked his head, sheltering the child with his body.

"Come on. You don't want to stay here, do you?" he asked, and the kid sniffed. "Come on. You can do this. Let's go."

After a slight hesitation, the child lifted its head and stared at him with giant blue eyes through whirling strands of hair. Between the tattered clothes and all the dirt, there was no way to tell if the little Underling was a boy or a girl.

"Hey, hi," Teddy said, brushing hair out of the child's face. "Don't worry." He took off his long-sleeved shirt. "Climb on my back, and we'll get out of here. You want to get out of here, yes?"

The kid nodded, sniffed, and crawled over to him. As the Underling wrapped thin arms around Teddy's neck, he draped the shirt around both of them and tied the sleeves across his chest. With the child secured, he crept back to the bridge.

"Coming back," he yelled to his father. "Hold on tight," he said to the child, whose grip tightened.

With his heart pounding, Teddy began to cross the boards. The hole in the floor continued down and down, a black pit leading to an unseen bottom. Pushing back his fears, he inched forward, eyes trained on the next move. The wood bowed more this time, due to the extra weight of the child.

"Oh, boy," Teddy muttered under his breath. The grip of the Underling made it difficult for him to breath, let alone swallow.

Beneath him, the makeshift bridge wobbled as the floor behind him began to break away. First one board slipped out from under his hand and fell away, dangling by the wire tethering it to the other planks.

He tried to keep going, but another panel let loose next, and he froze, precariously clinging to the final slat before it too gave way.

The child screeched in his ear as they swung down into the pit. They jerked to a stop as the wire went taut. Above them, Pa yelled and groaned as he hauled on the thin cable keeping them from plunging to their deaths.

Gut hurting from where the wire dug into his flesh, Teddy grabbed the cable and steadied them. His pants pulled tight against his groin and the little Underling clung so hard to his throat, spots appeared before his eyes.

"Pa? I have nothing to grab onto," he croaked as he worked a little space between his neck and the kid's fingers.

"Hold on," his father shouted, his voice strained. "Dorkas. Dorkas! Gah, he left."

As Teddy began to rise slowly, he reached overhead, trying to grab hold of the edge of the floor. Finally, he managed to make contact with the splintering wood. His father pulled and pulled while Teddy caught a hold of the platform with first his fingers, and then his hands. Grunting and straining, he gradually climbed to safety.

"It's okay; you can let go," he said, panting as he collapsed by his father, who sunk down beside him.

The little Underling squealed and let go, eyes as big as Teddy's hand. With another cry, the child bolted through the maze of wood and pipes before they could do anything about it.

"Well, at least the kid is safe," Pa said, grasping Teddy's shoulder. "Come on. Let's get back ourselves."

After a bout of coughing, Teddy cleared his throat and nodded. Limbs shaking, he wormed his way back through the criss-cross path of debris. Behind him, Pa followed with a little more difficulty and a lot more swearing.

"You okay back there?" he asked after a rumbling bang and a loud curse.

"Yeah," his father said with a grunt. "Damn pipe. My foot's caught."

"I'll come back and help," Teddy said, trying to figure out how to turn around in such tight corners.

"Teddy? You there?" called a voice from farther in front of him.

"Henri? Yeah. Hey, can you clear some of this out of the way? Pa's stuck," Teddy answered as he realized his only viable path was forward. He twisted and turned until he reached the place where their brute was pulling a large beam out of way.

"There you are," Henri said, his face lighting up with relief as he hauled Teddy to a standing position.

"Ah, huh," Teddy gasped, staggering. "Pa needs a little help though." He managed to wave in his father's direction before sinking down onto a broken desk.

Henri nodded and continued to create a larger opening until he reached Pa. After he freed Teddy's father's foot, the brute carried him out of the maze despite Pa's many protests.

"Did you see a little kid come through here?" Pa asked Henri as he mopped his forehead with his shirt.

"Uh, yep. Tiny thing ran past. Mrs. Peterson caught. All good. Saw creeper too. He duck fast like guilty rat. Thought I'd see what up to."

"We're glad you did," Teddy said as he massaged his neck. "Could have used you earlier, but all is well."

"Nice to know someone's safe," Pa said and glanced back at the maze as the floor shuddered. "Well, relatively anyway."

Teddy clasped his father on the shoulder and grinned. "Let's get out of here," he said and they staggered back toward the safer area of Undercity.

As they entered the area where the floor was more stable, a tremendous crash came from behind them along with a cloud of dust and dirt. Teddy froze, his heart jumping to his throat.

"We won't tell your Ma about this," Pa said, and Teddy nodded.

"Good idea."

Chapter 6

After Teddy located Jolon again, they worked for more hours than he could keep track of. All their neighbours pitched in moving rubble, digging people out, working on securing walls, and trying to salvage whatever they could of their Undercity crumbling around them.

"I'm tired," Jolon babbled as he trailed behind Teddy. "Tired, hungry tired, numb tired, and tired, tired." He sat down on a large boulder and tossed back some water from his canteen. Mud and muck streaked his face and stuck his curls upright. "I don't think we're going to find any more pockets."

"Yeah," Teddy sighed, sitting by his brother. "I'm so drained, my bones resolved to quit working, and my muscles agreed."

All around him, sweaty tattered people dug away with little air or light. "These are good people when the need is strong."

"Uh-huh," Jolon nodded. "And rotten when the need is ripe. Let's take bets on which need is more common."

"Ehh, you two are lazy," old man Fudge shouted at them as he went by with his cart overflowing with bags of clutter to sort and clean. His three sisters ambled along behind him, dragging their bodies as though they were ancient. He thrust a shovel at the mound behind them. "Dig, dig."

"Ahh, Fudge, you are an inspiration," Pa said as he joined them. "You put us all to shame."

The man's mouth spread into a display of rotting teeth. "I show you; I survive anything. Anything! No tunnel will do me in. I been down here all my life, can't read, can't write, but I survive. Don't need nuttin else. Just me."

"And us," one of his sisters said, poking him with a cane.

An' you lot. Don't get all pushy now." His voice drifted off as he went down the tunnel.

"Don't mind him, boys, you're doing terrific," Pa encouraged as he slumped down beside them.

"Pa, this won't work. We can't do this in secret," Teddy said as he stared at the people trying to survive in a place, in a state, no human should live in. There was little air or light, and the bodies were accumulating. He wanted to vomit.

His father tapped out a rhythm on the side of his leg. "I understand, but our choices are limited. For all we know we discovered all there is and anything else is buried."

"It isn't. There are ceiling windows everywhere and more space than we need to fit all Underlings and even some Upper- lords if we wanted to," added Jolon, bursting with excitement.

"Excuse me?" Pa said with a confused expression.

Teddy glared daggers at his brother.

"Sorry, just done, so done," he muttered, burying his head in his hands. "Ignore me. I babble."

"Teddy?" His father's eyes were pinpoint arrows of disapproval.

He squirmed, contemplating an elaborate story. "We, ummm, we went to Montgomery Mall last night," he said as he realized lying wouldn't help anyone.

"You, you..." He took a deep breath, his stern face scary. "You and you," he pointed to each one in turn, "went exploring alone. How? Henri and I..." Pursing his crooked lips, he stared at the place where the brute grasped a broken beam and hauled it away. "He helped, didn't he? That's the only way you might move the door. Of all the foolish... do I need to explain to you the dangers of going on your own? I thought you were old enough to understand."

This last part he said to Teddy; his face grew hot with shame.

"I'm sorry, okay?" he said, so weary he didn't want to be calm. "But I can't stand this. I can't handle sitting here watching us all turn into living corpses because a few people control everything. Things shouldn't be this way. Sunlight, life, water, it should all be ours. I can't take this, and I want change. Things must evolve or what's the point in existing?"

He held his father's gaze. "And you know it. What is the point of scrimping for leftover air and water, killing ourselves over the whims of others? You know it, Pa. I'm worn out. We're all exhausted, and we can't sneak about anymore or there won't be any of us left."

It took a moment for his father to respond, but he nodded. "So, windows in the ceiling? Well, this is good."

Jolon's face brightened. "Yes, you missed this amazing sunrise."

Their father raised his thick brow. "Sunrise? You witnessed a sunrise?"

Teddy chuckled. "Yep. The sky was gold and red before turning this soft blue colour. It was beautiful." "We can do it, can't we?" Pa asked, his voice quiet.

"Yes," he replied, the word almost choking in his throat.

"Oh, how sappy can people get? I'm too tired for this mushiness," Jolon moaned. "We've been up for almost a full day without so much as an hour's sleep." He drew a large gloop of mud out of his hair and tried to fling the glob away as it stuck to his fingers. "A lot of good my weekly bath did now. I am going to stink like this for the next week, and here you two are being all... all... yuck."

"Ahh, Jol, let's get you two home before you fall asleep right here," Pa said, getting up.

"Oh, shyza," Jolon moaned, standing, his hand on his lower back. "I think I lost twenty pounds in sweat." He hauled up his trousers to emphasize his point.

"When we get back home, I'm eating until I can't move. 'Course I'm numb now, so that won't mean much. Okay, until I regained the twenty pounds this torture took from me."

Teddy attempted to listen to Jolon ramble as they made their way home, but his brain was too fuzzy with fatigue. He didn't care about food; all he wanted was somewhere soft to plop on until he was no longer drooping. They stumbled in the house, and he realized Henri was not with them.

"Pa? Where's our brute?"

His father sighed as he sat at the table. "He didn't want to leave yet. He's still digging. I tried to get him to stop, but, well, he needs to work things out of his system before he'll be back." He shifted toward Ma, and she sat beside him. She appeared so depleted, so drained.

"We should all get some rest. I think we've done all we can for now," she told them with a heavy sigh.

"What?" Jolon exclaimed, his eyes wide. "Wait, wha... what, where's the food? Hungry... nothing but two potatocakes all day."

Their mother got up and embraced him. "I'm sorry, dear, we shared what we had for now to feed the survivors." Her voice broke as she held him tighter. "We are out at the moment. I'm sorry."

"Don't dismay, my boy. We'll get more tomorrow," Pa assured them with hugs. "There's always a way to find more. Let's go to bed."

Numb and foggy, Teddy stumbled toward his bedroom.

"No food," Jolon muttered as they shuffled to bed. "Rations gone, extras gone, and no credits to buy more." "It was a worthy cause," he said though the old terror of starvation threatened to resurface.

"Yeah, but what now?"

He went to his airbed and left his brother to his nightmares.

Morning came with a start when he dislodged himself from his hammock and slammed to the floor. Everything ached as he got up and stumbled into the kitchen, his throat sore and dry. All the lights were out except one little dot, which kept flicking on and off at the table. A disgruntled Henri sat playing with the handlight Pa had given him. The brute's face was bent with sorrow.

"Hey, Hen, you're back," he said, uncertain of how to approach the brute. He sat at the table and tapped an awkward rhythm on its surface. "Henri? You okay?"

Henri nodded then shook his head. "You own me; family owns me. Wot do I do?"

"We don't own you, buddy. You're your own person. We just hired you."

He shook his head again. "I not bright."

The brute spoke as though his words were difficult to say.

"I no schooling; I don't; I no understand much and I clumsy because I don't think. And I not good brute." He gave a bitter laugh. "I not mean. Wish I was. If I was mean, I... I... I go up to bullies, those..."

"Scumbags," he offered.

"Scumbags and rip heads off each until none left."

"That is a noble sentiment despite how bad it might sound."

Teddy jumped and turned to see his father resting his bent frame against the nearby wall. "Pa."

His father chuckled. "Didn't mean to intrude and startle you, but I couldn't rest either. Your mother went to sleep and I hope will stay in bed until she has rested."

He put a hand on Henri's shoulder and squeezed. "Don't worry, Henri. We understand. It hurts to witness this world go on this way, but what can a person do? Those people in Uppercity don't seem to possess compassion or empathy, or any awareness of the suffering they cause. Well, most of them don't. A few like Georges understand, but are too fearful and comfortable to do anything."

"They worse than others," Henri said.

"No, they just feel as powerless as we do. Who's to say who is to blame for our situation? Do we live as puppets of Upperlord bullies? Or do we give them power over us?"

"I always thought you wanted to be an Upper," Teddy admitted.

Pa's expression turned sour. "At one time I thought that was the solution. If I joined them, I might influence them, but now I don't think so."

"Then we defeat them," Henri said, his voice cold.

"And become them? Not an option I like. No, I think the boys are right. We have no alternative, but to alter our living arrangements."

"So, we're going back and see if we dreamed everything?" This time, it was Jolon who stumbled in. He shuffled over to Pa and hugged him.

"Yes, my sleepy one. I'm sure you didn't dream it. Might be our best option. If we can establish our own colony, we will have the leverage to coexist as neighbours with Uppercity. We are taking a chance, but I cannot picture any other choice."

He flipped open his well-supplied stash and rummaged around until he located a few cookies. "It's not much, but it will be a start," he said as he handed them each one. "Caden is too weak to come with us, and Deb is too young, but we can't leave them here by themselves, unprotected."

"I stay," offered Henri, his face solemn. "I keep safe."

Pa shook the man's hand. "I appreciate your help." He turned toward the others. "However, that does not solve the current problem of no food in this home. That must be our priority. Therefore, we will first make a visit to a friend or two. Jolon, please make certain all the stashes are prepared for a few days' journey," he said, handing him his sack.

"Fill the water containers and make sure the oxygen cylinders are at maximum. Plus, if you can find a few extra, throw them in, and make sure we take whatever batteries you can find. Dig into the new supply we brought back last time. We don't want to risk running out of light."

"Can't Teddy help me?" he asked with a groan.

"'Fraid not. He and Henri are going to accompany me to the Uppercity. We should be back in an hour or so, and, with luck, with some food for everyone. Now mind you, don't tell your mother where we've gone if she happens to get up. She's had enough upsets for quite a while and I don't want her to worry," he added as they left.

"So, are we going to visit Georges again?" Teddy asked, doing his best to keep up with his father. They had set such a pace to reach Uppercity he felt stitches in his side muscles.

"That's where we'll start," Pa said, passing the giant entrance. He paused and showed his travel permit to the sentry on duty before they went through as the guard opened the gate.

It was early morning now, and a gloomy glow touched Uppercity. No one was about. It was unsettling to realize this was the same sort of sunrise he witnessed the day before. The sunroom dawn had been so dramatic and bright. This one seemed dusty and dirty as though it was a leftover that slept under the mat all night.

"Where is everyone?" he whispered.

"They don't rise until near midmorning," Pa answered in a similar tone.

He wasn't sure what to think. It seemed like such a waste of time.

"Besides, the day is still new, and I don't think even you are up this early on a regular basis." He had a smattering of amusement in his voice, and Teddy chuckled.

"Guess so."

They wandered through the market where the shops were all shut up with curtains and boards covering their goods. The only other people around were a few brutes who stood guard and stared with suspicion as they passed. Teddy thought they were going to find Georges in the same place they had before, but instead of going to the auction pavilion they turned off a side street that ended at a simple door. Pa knocked, and they waited and waited. His father knocked again. Henri seemed to run out of patience, and he pounded on the wood, rattling the door on its hinges.

"Calm, Henri. Remember, she's our friend," Pa cautioned. "Remember, she was good to you."

The brute agreed with a reluctant grunt.

"I understand. You want the world to improve, but you need enough patience to let it evolve over at least a day. Otherwise, it won't be for the better, and the shock will cause havoc."

A small door to their left opened, and a face appeared: ugly and cross. "Yeha? Who are yeh and what de yeh want?"

"It's Peterson, Duras, I need to see your Lord."

"Eh, she's going te bed. Yeh too early."

"Come now, Duras," his father continued, holding out a necklace with a green bauble on it. Teddy recognized it as something they picked from the first store they inspected at the mall. "I brought you a present."

Her red, blue eyes went wide, and she reached for it through the tiny door with a wrinkled hand.

"Ah, ah, you must let us enter if you want it," he said, and she cast curse eyes at him, her mouth working over ugly, distorted teeth.

She shut the little door with a bang. They heard her clicking lock after lock before the door opened wide and she held out her hand. Pa dropped the necklace on her palm as they invaded Georges' home. She grasped her treasure and scurried away while he secured the door, turning the row of locks.

The room was grey except for a sliver of light filtering in through a half-covered window. Teddy peered through the glass, but all he discovered was a wall of dirt a few feet away, which went up and up.

He turned away.

Pa sat on an old armchair across from a couch. The lone figure of Georges lay on the dilapidated sofa, her hair askew and a bottle clutched in her hand. A dreadful noise similar to a dying motor emanated from her.

Henri hoisted one end of the chesterfield and dropped it. He shrugged and blushed as his father shook his head at him. "That's how she always had me wake her up," he explained and did it again.

This time, Georges snuffed and snorted before she half sat up. "Wha? Who, Duras, why are you letting riffraff in my home?" she bellowed as she glared at them. She rummaged under a cushion and wrenched out a lengthy blade, brandishing it. "Who are you and what do you want?"

"Georges, it's me, Truman. Stop with the knife. We're harmless."

"Eh? Duras, get me a damn light." She made an attempt at standing and fell back on the sofa.

Teddy lit a candle with a match from a pack sitting on the end table by his father's chair.

She held her hands over her eyes. "Ahg. Damn people don't realize it's too early to be visiting no matter who the hell you are."

Pa dropped a bottle in her lap. "Here, take a spot of what troubles ya. I'm in need of your assistance, and I need your head clear."

The woman glared, her nose scrunching as her lips squished together, but she snatched up the bottle and took a dramatic drink. She belched, dragging her shirt across her chin. "I don't take refunds on brutes," she said, eyeing Henri. "I told you he was a horrible brute when ya hired him."

"No, no, He's fine. It's another problem."

"The kid?" she asked, thrusting a finger Teddy's way, and he backed up. "I told you to hide 'im, charming thing that he is."

He had an urge to bathe as she scrutinized him.

"No, Georges, it's not Teddy either." His father leaned forward and caught her gaze. "You heard about the cave-in, yes?"

The Upperlord groaned and collapsed back in a listless heap. "Uhgh, Peterson, of course." She guzzled more wine. "It rumbled through Uppercity the instant it happened. You know as well as I do, no one up here is going to help. You must petition the council like every other Underling."

"Georges, you're not listening."

"No, Peterson, I'm not." She drank again and burped.

"We've had this conversation before. You seem to think I'm more concerned than I am and you seem to think you can hold that against me. Well, you can't. I'm as rotten as the rest of those rotten buggers, including my sister, who tell you what you can and can't do, and don't give a damn what happens to anyone else as long as they get their little piece of this pathetic society you call a world. So, you are whining to the wrong person. I'm scum and so is everyone else. You are talking to the wrong person." She hiccupped and lay back down, burying her head in a pillow.

Henri yanked the cushion away, pulling Georges back up to a sitting position. She stared at him, stunned.

"You converted my puffy bear," she protested. "You made a brute out of him. How dare you? I gave him to you 'cause you were supposed to save him from such a fate."

"Don't dismay, Georges, he's still a puffy bear; he's just done watching people die." Pa sat back with his usual grin back on his face. "You are a fake, Georges; you might hide in cynicism, but you are soft inside and you know it."

"Don't know what you're talking about," Georges objected with a pout.

"We don't need much from you at the moment; we just need some food."

The Upperlord narrowed her eyes as he studied Pa. "That's all? You're hungry? Well, no problem. The larder's over in the corner. Go snack on a cookie or something." She flopped back down again. "I think you might even find a few potatoes too. I'm not too fond of edibles, so there isn't much, but indulge in something."

"We don't need a snack; we need food, Georges, as much food as we can get. I have a family to feed."

Georges opened an eye, wide and buggy, and stared at him. "Oh, hell, you're serious."

"Yes, Georges, I am."

"What can you give me?"

His father brought out a hand-sized drawstring sack from his jacket. "How about these?" He poured out an assortment of jewellery across the table.

"Oh, double hell with pickles," she muttered under her breath. "Where did you get those?" She tugged a necklace from the pile and the gold chain shimmered in the candlelight. "I haven't seen anything this good in years. There hasn't been anything this good in ages. Even Madame Belle has run out of pieces of such worth. Where?"

"We scrounged it."

"You scrounged it." Georges nodded. "This kind of thing is not something you dig out of this pit of a world. I know. Anything worthwhile was collected years ago. Where are you getting this? Is there more? This is quality, Peterson, this... this... this is why you wanted a brute, isn't it? You found a trove, and you need a brute to protect it, and I gave you the puppy brute. Damn." She thrust her boney body up from the couch and paced, running her fingers through her hair and tugging at her arms.

"Damn, damn. This is dangerous. Don't you understand? People here will take this from you without giving anything in return. They don't want you up here, Peterson. I told you before; they don't want anyone else up here, not even each other. They're greedy and bored. They will take you and your family apart if they even suspect you found something extraordinary."

"Calm yourself, Georges. I understand." Pa got up and put a hand on Georges' arm. "This is why I came to you. I need your assistance. This is a down payment. Between you and me we can maneuver this so nobody will realize anything until it is too late, but for now, I need food."

"Oh, hell, Tru, you're trusting me." She threw a hand above her head. "That is such a bad idea. Why, how can you even think confiding in me is a good idea?"

"Because I know you, Georges. I know you better than you want me to, and you know that. You don't like this world any more than I do. The only difference is you gave up searching for a solution whereas I still believe in the possibility of a new life. So, I trust you. I have to. This is the truth. My allies are rare, and you have always been good to me. You possess a heart. You hide in a bottle and pretend you're terrible. Well, this is your chance to be what you are, a good person."

"Bite your tongue," Georges shouted, horrified. "That is a lie, a horrible lie... oh, hell...." Her words petered off as she slumped in defeat. "Fine. I don't believe you, but I'll humour you for now."

"Thank you."

"Wait here. I'll... I'll see what I can do."

Chapter 7

What a dump. That was the best compliment Teddy could come up with for Georges' place. In the past hour, while they waited, he searched through bags of bottles, stacks of illegible notes, and too many piles of soiled clothing.

"Pa? Is this what Upperlords do? Drink and make a mess?"

His father twirled a decanter in his hand. "I'm afraid so. Well, at least, that's what Georges does. I don't know too much about the others except for rumours from cleaning staff and such."

"Where do they get all the alcohol? I thought the original stash of booze ran out several years ago."

"This is filth brewed by Upperlords, themselves." He peered closer at the words scrawled across the label. "In fact, I think this might be Georges own stock. It is most often made with potatoes."

"I'm sick of potatoes," Teddy sighed and stared out the window at the wall of dirt.

"Me too," agreed Henri, his chin resting on his hands.

"I get they are the staple of our lives because they are simple to grow in this underground prison, and they make flour..."

"Alcohol," his father added.

"Soup," Henri said.

Teddy put his head on his hands. "Okay, yes, you can use them for almost anything, but don't you ever imagine what an apple pie would be like?"

Their brute blinked and stroked his chin. "What's an apple?"

"It's a round, crisp... thing... fruit." He struggled to answer what he had only read about. "They're good, or so I read."

"You depend on too many books, my boy," Pa said, patting him on the leg. "What is the point of craving something you only read about? All that does is make one pine for what they don't own and hate what they need."

"I could devour potato raw now," Henri sighed, rubbing his stomach.

"Or fried. Tisha makes wonderful fried potatoes with a spiced portion of dried chicken mixed in. Not always easy to find spices, so she saves it for special occasions."

"I like it when she shreds carrots in them too," Teddy admitted as he gave in and realized he would inhale almost anything edible to stop his stomach from complaining.

"How we get chickens?" Henri asked. "They pets at first, like dogs and cats, or what?"

"My old teacher said when they planned out the domed city designed to save everyone and everything, they had different sections devoted to other animals, but they all collapsed aside from three greenhouses and the chicken farm," Teddy explained, trying to ignore the knots convulsing his stomach. Fatigue and hunger made him a little punchy. "Some people eat them."

"Chickens, yes we know, Ted," Pa said. "You eat them yourself."

"No, cats and dogs." He yawned until his jaw cracked.

"Ah, yes. Mrs. Fish trapped a couple of mutts the other day and is going to try to breed them. She's hoping to get into the meat market and make pelts out of the fur. She thought about trying to breed Critter and Stub, but apparently they're getting too old."

Somehow the idea nauseated Teddy. The dogs were not his favourite friends, but they loved the family. Plus, he read too many stories about people and their faithful pets, and always thought it wasn't a good plan to eat the one you love.

Henri exhaled, his barrel chest deflating. "I want one when young. Wanted one to play with and be with. Didn't have anyone else after Keme left and they... petable, kittens too, petable." He made a motion as though he was stroking an animal.

"I think we're all getting sleepy," his father said, yawning too. "I'm going to raid her stores and see if I can't come up with something to give us a little energy."

"Henri, what happened to your family?" Teddy asked after his father went into another room.

The brute stared with bleary eyes before hugging himself. "Don't think ever had any. I get I had beginning, baby me, but I shift from person to person. Then no one. Just me. Others died or disappeared, or stopped finding me useful."

Teddy understood. "Yeah, never liked being shuffled about much."

"You too, huh? They not parents?"

"Not my original parents," Teddy admitted. "They're the first people to stay, though, and they don't ask anything of me. I help out of want, not their need."

"Good people," he said, staring after Pa. "Sensed that; good people." He turned toward Teddy with hope lurking in his eyes. "They keep me?"

He whacked the brute in the shoulder. "I told you, we don't own you; we hired you."

Henri frowned at this.

"Yes, Henri, they will keep you for as long as you want."

A grin blossomed on his face. "K."

"How about some beets and eggs?" his father asked as he rejoined them with two plates piled high with food.

The aroma almost put Teddy on the floor as he salivated. "Beets? Oh, yes. I haven't had beets in ages." He got up and took the plates from his father and distributed them. Pa handed each one of them a fork, grinning.

"Let's not concern ourselves with manners, boys. Dig in."

Henri chuckled, and Teddy grinned, taking in a giant mouth full. The flavour was fantastic, sweet and juicy, and they devoured the lot in moments. Full, they sat back, rubbing their bellies.

"Is there some we can bring everyone else, some beets or something?" he asked, feeling a trace guilty knowing they were hungry back at Undercity.

His father was about to answer when a commotion at the door cut him off, and Georges burst in pushing a cart filled with sacks.

"All right, you thieves and scroungers. Here's the deal." She parked her load and flopped in a chair, whipping her hair out of her way. "I give you this food, and you take me to where you got this treasure."

Teddy turned to his father. They needed the supplies, but taking an Upper to the mall was a risk.

His father sat back and pondered Georges.

"Come now, Tru, you don't have much choice. I promise I will keep everything a secret. I want to understand what I'm getting myself into. You're asking a lot of me." She flourished a hand toward the cart.

"This is a risk. Purchases such as this get noticed, and people ask questions. I don't own brutes. Never wanted 'em; never needed 'em. My sister deals with those issues. Now you ask me to take risks, and I believe I deserve to know what I'm letting myself in for."

After a moment, Pa nodded. "Fine."

"Pa."

His father put up a hand. "I know, Teddy, but change doesn't come without risk, and she's right, we have no choice."

"Good," Georges clapped her hands together and rubbed them. "Now, let's go before I rethink this or Duras comes back and squeals to my sister."

She shoved the cart. "Henri, if you wouldn't mind. My old back has had enough of experiencing hard labour."

As Teddy held the door open, the brute passed with the mound of food—at least enough for a week if not two.

"Ma will love this."

Pa shook hands with Georges. "Let's hope so."

"Carrots, carrots, carrots," a happy Deb shouted as she danced about the cart when they got back. "And eggs, oh eggs. Ma? Scrambled? I adore them scrambled." She ran over to Georges and attached herself to the Upper lord's bony knees.

"Thank you, thank you. My tummy says thank you."

Georges managed a crooked smile and detached her. "Yes, well, your tummy's welcome. Um, erg, child."

"Deb, her name is Deb," their mother said, her voice testy. She was not pleased to see an Upperlord in their home, but the load of food made her more receptive despite herself.

"Yes, love, I'll scramble the eggs." She gave her a gentle, but firm shove toward the back rooms. "Now, wake your brother and sister. I'll get this all going and we'll feast."

"Yah," she cheered and dashed from the room.

"I thought Jolon was getting the stashes ready," Teddy said to his father.

"He was," Ma said. She put her hands on her hips and frowned at each one of them in turn. "I don't know what you four are planning, but I sent him back to bed. What? Were you going to drop off the food and leave me a note? It's a good thing Deb only sleeps for ten minutes at a time, or I would have woken up to an empty house."

Pa swept her up in his arms despite her protests. "Tisha, my love, all will be well; you'll see." He wiped her cheek and gave her a kiss.

"Oh, yes, you brought an Upperlord into my house. Sorry, Georges, but I don't have much use for your kind at the moment."

She bowed. "Don't fear, my dear, I don't have much use for my kind at any time, so we both agree."

Her words did not quite remove the disapproval from their mother's countenance, but Georges did manage to elicit the hint of a grin. "Fine. You get ready, and I'll make you some food."

"We've eaten," Teddy admitted though he regretted speaking as her attention went to him.

"Oh, you have? Eating with the posh Upperlords now? Well, I shall feed the others a humbler fare, shall I?"

"The meal was humble, Ma. Don't be mad. Pa cooked, and we were so hungry."

"Yes, and they didn't even offer me any," Georges said, sighing with a most sorrowful pout.

"Well, you sit, and I'll show you what true food is like," she said, offering Pa's stool.

The Upperlord nodded, her braids wagging with the motion, and she perched on the seat, trying to tuck her legs underneath. "Would be delighted, my lady. Would be most delighted."

Pa beckoned to Teddy, and they left the main space.

"Don't worry about your Ma," his father said as he chose an oxygen tank and stuck it in his stash. "She'll be all right. She is a little weary, like the rest of us."

"Can we leave them alone, Pa?"

"They'll be fine, Ted, but we'll haul the doors closed in case. I think I might even get Mrs. Fish's brood over as well." He handed his stash to Teddy.

"You finish putting this together, and I'll go round her up. After, we'll secure the gate to the bridge. Everyone will be snug until we come back."

"So, we're going?" Jolon asked when Teddy came back into the house. He was busy demolishing a large plate of eggs and mashed potatoes.

"Yeah," he said, sitting on his chair. He took the cup of water his mother offered and downed it. "We're going to fix the world. Not sure if I'm excited or terrified."

"The canteens filled with enough water?"

"Yes, Ma."

"You're going to need several to keep going for a few days. You better take Henri to carry things."

"Pa wants him to stay here and protect you."

"Protect me... from what? With the bridge secure, no one can get in. You're taking Henri and all his brawn, and that's final." She whirled around and took a tray of cookies from the oven. "Now, you get the blue container and fill it with these as soon as they're cool. This is the best food to bring on these trips and I don't want any of you starving either."

Teddy did as his mother commanded and the others kept to themselves. He understood she was only worried, but it was not good to antagonize her further by making light of the situation. He let his father deal with his mother and the whole issue with Henri. The addition of Mrs. Fish did sound like better protection than Henri. She had a reputation for her solid constitution and accurate aim with a stick while her husband and sons preferred slings and rocks.

"Caden better?" Henri asked as he added his plate to the cleaning bucket.

Ma stroked his cheek. "Yes, dear, she is much better today. I think she'll be on her feet soon."

He held out a part of a yellow flower he had somehow plucked from Uppercity. "Found in crack. You give her?"

She took his offering with a gentle smile. "Thank you, Sweetie, you are so generous." She gave him a kiss on the cheek, and he blushed.

"Well, a brute with a sweetheart. What other wonders are in the world?" Georges asked as Teddy and Jolon made gagging gestures.

"Be kind," their mother ordered as she left with a plate for Caden. "And mind the food or you'll be eating burnt biscuits for the next few days."

"So, this is your grand secret," Georges said upon arriving at the mall. "Well, well. A whole new possible situation, a completely new city." She sniffed the air. "Well, it's breathable." She sniffed again. "In fact, it is quite fresh." "Fresh and invigorating," Pa replied with his wacky grin. "Interesting, right?"

"There's more," Jolon piped in.

"Lots more," Teddy added, and they both grinned.

"Yes," Pa said with a disapproving shake of one crooked finger. "These little gophers snuck in the other night and went exploring farther than they should have. Well, go on, grab courage and lead. Show us what you rats found."

"Rat isn't bad if you can get a hold of enough potato juice to drown your taste buds in," Georges said with a slap to Henri's shoulder.

He pulled at his ragged fleece shirt and sighed. "Good with onions if ya kin get em, onions." Teddy shuddered.

"You ever eat 'em?" Jolon asked, his face tinted green as they guided the others.

"No. Almost did, though. About a week or so after my parents died. The guy down the way ate them every day. He had a special way of catching them—traps he made himself out of bits of wire and other objects. He'd hang them from a rack he had secured to this little hovel he lived in. The place stunk and was disgusting to look at, and he'd build this fire under 'em to singe the hair off and dry them out."

"That's gross," Jolon said, shivering. "But I remember rubbish like that. I was nonstop scared, and I don't even remember why I was alone. One day I had a mom and the next I didn't. I scrounged for anything I could find. I tried bugs once and worms more than a few times. I guess that's why I can't seem to stop eating now."

Putting an arm around his younger sibling, Teddy laughed. "You're safe. It's all good now. You and me, we've got family and," he turned them around to get a view of the full expanse of the area, "all the potential of a new home. Imagine. This could be a place with food enough for everyone. Where families stay together and children grow up healthy."

"You're such a dreaming dope," Jolon said, pushing him, but he grinned.

"Yeah, well, you're a weird freak of nature."

"Oh, funny, is that the best you can do?"

"Nope, but I'm not gonna waste my best on an annoying little brother like you," he replied and whistled as he sauntered ahead.

"Hey, not too fast," his father called out, as Jolon took off after Teddy. "We still don't know what's out here."

"What's out here?" Georges asked, her face glistening with sweat. "What could be out here?"

"Not much," Pa said.

"Just goblins," Jolon said.

"And trolls," Teddy added.

"What trolls?" Henri asked with a worried expression.

"Boys, don't be troublesome," their father said. "We face enough real troubles down here without making up new ones. Relax, Georges, Henri. There shouldn't be anything worse than snakes and rats, but we have found ratdogs and the odd alligator in the sewers. Can't say if they are in these parts, but it never hurts to keep an eye out."

"Lovely," Georges groaned. "How about rest and food?" She scooped a tiny glass box from the ground. "I would not mind a moment to explore some of these stalls."

"Oh, no, we haven't even come near the best part yet," said Jolon.

Teddy nudged him in the ribs.

"Ow, what?"

"Nuthin, except you're babbling." he said, trying to be subtle.

Pa patted him on the shoulder. "Calm, Teddy, we agreed to share everything with Georges."

"Yes, it seems, your father wants to trust me." She winked at him. "But don't you do that. Don't you follow his standards; you construct your own. It's a good survival trait in this world."

"Thank you, Georges, for such terrible advice. I would like my children to grow up a little less jaded if you don't mind."

The Upperlord snorted. "Bad idea, Tru."

Teddy wasn't certain whether the woman was joking or not, but he figured it wasn't important. He would go along with his father, but he would only trust so far.

"Fine," he said, at length and gestured to their left. "We go down this hall, and there's a door to our best find."

"The sunrise room?" his father asked, his voice holding a hint of excitement.

"Sure, if you want. Works for me," Jolon said. "Not bad at all."

"Accurate," Teddy said. "All right. Let's go."

A while later they sat in the same spot as last time, staring up at a blue sky.

"This is paradise," Pa said in a tone of awe, and he agreed. "This is amazing," Georges said, her gaze glued to the endless sky above. "This is more light than the entire Uppercity gets, except for the greenhouses. They're well defended, though. Protective, greedy buggers don't like to let anyone in."

"Paradise needs a cleaning," Teddy said, gesturing toward the tables and stalls. Faded pictures and signs curled away from the cement walls and pillars, and garbage lay scattered everywhere as though people left in a hurry.

"So this is a f... f... foo... food court," Jolon said, pointing up to a sign hanging from a beam high above them.

"Good, Jol. Yes, this is where people came for food," Pa said, turning a tray over in his hands. "This is good. This has some potential. Not certain what for, but I'll get to that later."

Jolon tugged on Teddy's sleeve and motioned toward one of the booths. "Come on."

"Check for cooking oil," Pa said. "These places should have a good supply, enough to keep us going for quite a while."

They rushed over to one of the stalls, and his brother flipped up a part of the disgusting counter to get in behind. It was a stinking mess of mould and grime.

"Looks like we have oil and lots of it like Pa thought," Teddy said, searching through a couple of cupboards. He pulled out two hefty jugs and stuck them on the cleanest part of the filthy surface.

"Okay, so the only things feasting here are bugs," He edged his way past an indistinguishable lump and got the nauseating sense at one time it wasn't food.

"I don't want to know," Jolon said, and they chose to go back. "Well, if there was anything edible here, it turned to insect food forever ago. Can't even find new bugs. Just empty shells," he said with a dejected slump to his shoulders. He sat down at one of the cleaner tables and Pa threw him a cookie.

"Eat up. I think I might even have some boiled eggs in here," he said as he dug through his equipment.

"So, I don't get it," Teddy said, taking a canteen of water and a biscuit. "My teacher said the whole world knew this disaster was coming, and they prepared by building the domes and stockpiling food and water. So, how come people went on like it was nothing? I mean, if I knew something was going to happen to change the existence of the entire world, I don't think going shopping would be high on my list that day."

"No, mine either," his father said. "But people are strange creatures, and there's no telling what they'll do."

Georges laughed. "That's right, Tru. You can't tell what they will do, and that is part of the problem."

The Upperlord accepted a cookie from Pa and munched it down. After, she brought out her canteen and took a swallow.

"See, they set everything up, so everyone assumed they were secure, so they went on with their day. They went shopping, and ate food, and had babies, and went to school, to work, and to wherever they went to fill up the hours of their days. Only when it hit, did they stop everything and stare up at the domes as wave after wave of volcanic lava, mud, and water pounded against them and go 'my isn't that interesting?' No, they panicked and rioted, breaking things and each other in their fear. They thought their seismic devices would stabilize the earth's crust and keep the damage to a minimum, but nature is a fickle thing and did not listen. Hence, more panic. Hence, people went mad."

With a dramatic stretch, Georges stuck her feet on another chair. She took another swig from her canteen and belched.

"See, this is the problem with the human race, we're all off balance when you come right down to our inner workings. We devour each other alive if it's a choice between death and life."

Pa snatched the jug from Georges' hand. "That's enough." He took a sniff of the stopper and made a face as he poured the liquid out on the soil.

"Just as I thought. No more, Georges. The last thing we need is you drunk." He tossed her back her empty bottle. "The days of cannibalism are over. They ended when people got over their fears and organized themselves."

"Yes, into Upperlords and Underlings," she sneered. "And tell me, Tru, if that is so good, why are you here with your ragtag group of pathetic orphans trying to find a happier life? People still feed on each other, Tru; they just do it a little slower than before."

"We're here because people can be better than that," Pa said. "Not everyone panics. Not everyone thinks of only themselves regardless of the cost to anyone else."

"And you believe this."

"Yes, Georges, without question, I do. Despite what happened or what will happen. This is what I believe." A glint sparked in the Upper's eyes as though she had been testing Pa and liked his answers.

"So, why so many died; panic?" Henri asked in a soft voice.

"Yep." She and Pa stared at each other, and the Upperlord broke into a broad smile. "They panicked, but we don't need to." She did a little dance and giggled. "We have time... time to build a new world. Nothing can get worse than it already is." Holding out her hand, she turned to him. "Right, Tru?"

They clasped hands and shook. "You are an odd one. Yes. It can't get any worse."

He clapped his hands together; the sound echoed off the surrounding brick. "Right. Let's set up camp, shall we? This courtyard will make a fine base, I think. I promised your mother I would find her a good home to move to if we do. So, let us put on our gloves and masks, find the stall, the most hideous stall, and shove all this mess in there. We'll seal the room up and see if we can't make the rest of this place liveable. My hope is this place hides water around somewhere, and I'm determined to find it. Jolon, you'll work with Henri and me; Teddy you take the other side with Georges."

Teddy took his synthetic gloves out of his stash's outer pocket. As a scrounger, he always had them with him and an extra pair just in case, which he handed to Georges.

"Here, you'll need these," he said as the woman stared at him as though he had two heads. "You wanted to be all in, right? Well, this is all in. They're not much, but they will protect you from a certain amount of germs and such." He passed her a white cloth mask too. "You'll want to use this against anything airborne. Not that it helps with everything, but it is better than breathing in junk, and it saves the oxygen tanks for emergencies."

The Upperlord took the supplies with some reluctance and put them on. "I would protest, but I fear it would be pointless. However, I would like to lodge a complaint none-the-less."

"If it makes you feel better."

"Yes, it does."

Teddy patted her arm. "Go ahead."

She laughed. "You are priceless. I think I'm going to like you despite myself."

Hauling himself on one of the counters, he grimaced at the disgusting oily dirt covering the surface. He shoved aside a large box to let Georges in.

"Oh, good. That is comforting. Don't like many people despite yourself, do you?"

She laughed again. "No, not many. Doesn't pay. Almost always ends in disaster."

They pushed the carton out into the centre and made their way into the back room. This one didn't seem to be too bad. There was still dirt and mould everywhere, but no mounds or strange remains. Teddy opened a tall cupboard, hoping he wouldn't find anything nasty inside. A broom and mop fell out, and he jumped back.

"Careful, those might clean you to death," Georges said while she rummaged through another shelf.

"Oh, funny. Spend a while thinking that one up, or was that off the tip of your tongue?"

"Ah, I don't believe in rehearsing my humour... takes the edge off."

He handed her the broom. "Enjoy."

She stared at it as though it was a foreign object. "What do you want me to do with this?"

"Go clear out the front," Teddy said, waving her away.

"Clear the front? And what are you going to do?" She held the broom at an arm's length.

"Don't whine." He handed her a box of plastic bags, which seemed to be in good shape. "I'm going to try to tidy up this back. If we're lucky, I'll find some cleaners that are still useable since we have no water. You'll need to triple the bags to make them strong enough to hold anything. Throw out anything too caked in mould to salvage."

She cocked her head to the side and knitted her eyebrows together. "Who put you in charge?"

He straightened up. "Do you know what needs to be done? Do you know how to handle bottles of cleaning supplies ready to burst at the lightest touch?"

"No," she admitted and wagged a boney finger toward him. "But I didn't come to be part of the sanitation crew. I came as an investor on a sightseeing tour."

"What do you think you're involved in?" he demanded with a shake of his head. "This isn't a business. This is survival."

"My dear boy, all business is survival, and all survival is business. Anyone who thinks otherwise is into religion, and that is a whole different business."

Exasperated, he turned back to his cupboards. "Just go."

The Upperlord left, grumbling, and Teddy found the cleaning supplies he was hoping for. Most of the bottles burst years ago and spread their contents everywhere. They mixed and corroded the wood before drying up into crystalline puddles. He grabbed a few bags and tripled them up before throwing away whatever he could.

It was a tedious afternoon and by the time they took a break, it seemed as though they achieved little. Georges surprised him by working hard and doing the worst tasks although she did not stop grumbling whenever he came near. They chose the stall Jolon and Teddy first explored to dump everything since it had a rolling aluminum door they could pull down to seal it off, and no one wanted to touch the lump of remains.

He folded out his sleeping mat. "Pa, we'll be at this forever if we don't find some water to assist us."

His father stretched out on his makeshift bed. "Tomorrow, we'll split up, and you and I can search for water while the others keep going here."

Teddy turned toward Georges, half expecting the Upperlord to complain, but she was snoring. His brother rolled his eyes and gazed upward, knowing it was useless to object. He stretched out too despite how hard the floor was, put his hands behind his head, and stared at the vast expanse above him.

"What are those?" Jolon asked, pointing a thick finger to the sky.

"Don't know. Lights of some kind," he answered, watching the pinpoint lights appear all over the dimming sky. "So this is night."

"It's Twilight," his father said, sighing. "Magical, isn't it?"

He drifted off, dreaming of a world without walls and windows.

Chapter 8

"So, I figure water flows downward, so... so... sooooo... where do we go?" Pa asked as they left the food court.

"We could check that?" Teddy suggested, noticing a filthy stand with a diagram like a map peeking out from under the dirt.

"Yeah, we could," his father replied with a pleased expression.

They hurried over and wiped away a layer of dust. "Here we are," he said, jabbing a finger on the tiny sign declaring 'you are here.' He traced over the red lines, which spread out every which way. "This place is huge. If these places are all useable, we might fit everyone and their pets."

"Don't get too excited, my boy. So far, luck is trotting along with us, but the chance of this whole place being accessible is a tad much to hope for."

"How do you do it, Pa?"

"Do what?"

"Flip from 'we've got miracles happening all around us' to 'don't get your hopes up.'"

His father laughed. "Depends on how hungry I am. The world can appear rosy or gloomy depending how full my stomach is. Now, according to this, there are levels further down. This has potential. What do you say we search for one of these stairwells and explore?"

"Fine, but I'm bringing lots of cookies," Teddy said. He gestured to the path on his left. "I think we go this way."

"So, what do you think of Georges?" his father asked as they went.

"She's interesting."

"Interesting... hmmm, and cryptic. In what way?"

"In the—I don't know if I trust her, and I'm not sure I want to because she seems shallow and self-absorbed—way."

"That is what she wants everyone to believe. That is her defense mechanism... her protection. She is quite intelligent and caring. She just doesn't want anyone to know. Comes from having to survive with her sister. Belinda is a cold person. She'd kill Georges if she found out she came here."

"So, won't she be suspicious when Georges doesn't appear today?"

"No, she often disappears in a moping, alcoholic funk for days at a time. Her sister won't miss her for at least three or four more days. Here we go," his father finished, pointing to a large double door.

They donned their oxygen masks, and he nodded as his father glanced at him before pushing the door open. It moved slowly, but easy, surprising both of them. He entered first, flicking on his lantern. Their footsteps echoed as they went. He paused at the next landing and went to inspect the door, but his father stopped him and pointed downward, so he went on. Two more landings and two more doors later, he wondered how far down the place went. His mask itched and his breath created moisture, tickling his nose. He wanted to check the air, but his father kept them going until they reached an impasse.

Teddy checked his meter, which read as borderline, but breathable. He slipped his respirator off and studied the steps below. "Water?" He stared at the brackish pool filling the stairwell.

"Water," his father repeated. "Now, what do you think, drinkable or poisoned muck to strip your insides? He rubbed his hands together. "This might be good." His father slung off his stash, flipped back the flap, and fished out his water tester. It was a crude system he fixed after an Upperlord had tossed it away.

"Well?" he asked while his father scooped some of the liquid up and tipped a few chemicals in. "Wait."

He stopped breathing.

His father's shoulder's slumped in disappointment. The water in the vial turned a putrid green. "Not so much. Well, we keep searching."

Exhaling, Teddy swiveled around, trying to decide which way to go. "Where to? We either go back up or through that way." He indicated the door to his left. "Masks on, dear boy, and forward."

He grinned at his father, donning his mask before checking the levels on his gauge. Afterwards, he pushed against the door. It opened part of the way with a scraping protest, which crept down his spine.

Wary, he slipped in. Darkness obscured the dank space that echoed with the slightest noise. He shivered as the chill of the room wrapped around him and cut through the cloth of his shirt, his t-shirt, and into his skin. Pa tapped him on the back and removed his respirator. The air smelled rancid with the heavy weight of oil and rust.

"Not the greatest, but breathable. Keep your meter on to signal for dead pockets. Damn, it's cold." He lifted his light higher. The place was almost empty.

Teddy studied the lines marking the floor and making stalls everywhere. A rusted, dented sign dangled from a bolt on a pillar. "Parking level C, what kind of place is this?"

"A parking garage. Didn't any of your books mention them? No? Well, they are not exciting. People parked their cars here."

"Cars. What a strange idea. Yeah, they're a great resource for us for fuel and oil now, but I can't picture ever needing one. Can you imagine going so far you needed something other than your feet to get there with?" Teddy said as the biting air made him wish he brought a coat.

"Wouldn't mind one for the journey here," his father admitted.

"They'd never get over the bridge—too much junk in the way. Do you ever crave for open space, Pa?"

"Oh, yes. I have dreamt about vast expansive fields ever since I was younger than you. My father shared tales about the past, the same tales his grandfather told him."

"He was one of the original survivors, right?"

"Yes, he was but a baby when everything changed. Now, everything is only stories his Pa passed down, and my Pa told me when I was so small."

"You are lucky you knew your extended family."

His father gave him a side hug. "He would have liked you lots, my Pa would."

"Do you think we'll ever live beyond walls, or do you think this is life now?"

"Hmmm. I'm ever hopeful, Teddy, ever hopeful. Still, does it matter? All we got is now, and so this must be our joy. You all are my joy, you, Caden, Deb, Jolon, and your mother. Every moment I am thankful for each of you because otherwise I would be worse than Georges; old, cynical, afraid, and living an empty existence watching life go by and yet unwilling to alter anything."

"She is here, though, now, helping us. That is progress."

He stopped and stuck out his chin, running a hand through his stringy hair. "This is true." The beam from his light danced about as he swept the room. "Look."

Teddy raised his handlight to where his father indicated. At first, he wasn't certain what he was in front of him—the whole area was so black and empty. Next, he perceived it was an extensive pool of water as the light glistened on the rippling surface.

"More water," his voice dropped out of reverence before something precious. "Do you think it's deep?"

They inched towards the edge, testing each step in case of a fault in the ground. Pa crouched and found a piece of stone and tossed it in the pool. The pebble sploshed and sent out ripples before settling again.

"So far so good."

Grabbing his father's arm, Teddy paused. "You don't think there's anything in it, do you?"

"Can't tell, not sure," Pa said, shrugging. "Still, I survive by being paranoid, and one never can say. First thing to do is test for quality. After, we'll test if it's safe."

He didn't like the sound of that any more than he liked the idea of getting closer to the lagoon. It was so dark and still, and the place was eerie. They stared at the water, neither one moving. He nudged his father.

"You first."

"Maybe we should...."

"I doubt it's any good."

"Yes, perhaps we should leave it alone."

"Good idea."

They took an involuntary step back.

"This is water—gallons and gallons of water. More water than I've ever seen in my life, Teddy." "Nothing to be afraid of."

His father shook himself. "Right. What could be in there? This place is deserted with nothing for anything to live off that we know of." He removed his stash and pulled out his kit. "So, let's check if we can drink it. If this is good, we may have enough here to supply everyone."

Teddy shone some light around, scoping the area as his father worked. The pool seemed to extend about thirty feet in both directions with a long ledge that disappeared into shadows on the far side. He turned his handlight toward the water, trying to penetrate the depths, but it seemed endless. Something flashed in the corner of his vision. It glimmered for a moment and was gone.

"Pa? Did you see that?"

"Huh? What?"

"Something's shiny is in the water. At least, there was."

His father peered at where the light hit. "Might be a pipe," he said. He mumbled under his breath as he put his equipment away. "There are lots of pipes and other waste. This is undrinkable at the moment—too much oil and such—probably from cars. The best we can hope for is to be able to use it for such things as cleaning and sewage."

"I'm not taking a pee in there," he said, backing away as something glimmered again. "Something is moving under the surface, and I'm not going to bare anything valuable as bait."

"Ah, Teddy, you're getting ahead of yourself. We'll get some more lights down here later and see what we can make of things. You never know, we might be able to get some steam energy happening to make life a little easier." He straightened up and stretched his back, turning away from the water.

"In the meantime, let's keep searching. There's another door over in that direction and, oh, hell!"

Teddy whirled around at his father's yell and faced a ratdog larger than any they had ever encountered before. The creature's eyes glimmered yellow in the light, and its teeth glinted with ugly stains of brown as it bared them in a rictus snarl.

"Oh, damn," he gasped, backing up, his hand going to his knife.

Another ratdog joined the first, their cone heads down low ready to attack. They stank like rotting food. Teddy clutched his blade in his hand and crouched down.

His father yanked out his knife. "No sudden moves. I'll draw them this way while you try to get behind them. With any luck, we'll..." He got no further as the nearest ratdog screeched and charged. His father whirled and struck. The creature yelped, but tried to sink its teeth into Pa's arm.

Teddy scrambled to help his father, but the second ratdog cut him off. He wrenched around as the beast went for his leg. His heels touched the edge of the pool, and he tried to stop himself from falling in, but the animal lunged forward, and he went backward. Water swirled around him as he went under and everything went dark. Indiscernible tentacles wrapped around his legs, he broke the surface for a moment gasping for air before he went under again. The more he fought, the more entangled he got. His lungs burned, but he could not reach the surface again. A strong force yanked him downward. Every part of him screamed for air, but there was none.

At the moment he thought he would never breathe again, he hit a ledge. Thrashing about, he seized a pipe, hauling himself upward. At least, he hoped he was going upward. He was so disoriented, he wasn't sure, but somehow he surfaced with a wrenching gasp. Coughing and wheezing, he dragged himself to shallow ground and lay still, unable to move anymore. Water ran out of his mouth with every cough. He blacked out.

He didn't know how much time had gone by when he regained consciousness, but he was grateful he did. Shaking, he crawled further onto the cement floor and sat shivering, and thanking the universe, and whomever else he could think of, he was still alive. He lost his light and soaked the contents of his stash. Wherever he was, he could breathe, and the area seemed to be well lit.

"So, you're all right?"

He pivoted around at the sound of the rich, feminine voice. She stood by him with a floor-length dress on and extensive hair twisted up in a heavy bun, and a beautiful golden dog by her side. Her complexion was rusty and freckled. She seemed about the age of his mother; he guessed by the grey hair and the wrinkles around her cedar-brown eyes. She was smiling at him with a full set of teeth most Uppers would envy.

"Uh, um..."

"You do speak, yes? You sputtered some choice words when I hauled you out."

Shivering, he backed away, but the pool was behind him, so he huddled in a ball. "Yes, I speak. You got me out?"

"Of course, me and Toro here." She scratched behind the dog's ear, and its tongue lolled about. "Otherwise that current would have pulled you under and who knows where you would have ended up."

"Mmmmy fffather," he gasped, his teeth chattering. "The ratdogs. I need to...."

"You need to get warm," she interrupted as she threw a blanket around his shoulders. "Come on, stop your shaking and get under this cover. I got a fire going at my hovel and a crumb of tasty food. I'll see to your father. Where was he? Up the channel? Not a good place to be."

Teddy's stomach betrayed him at the thought of something to eat, grumbling with vigour. He let her drag him away, his head heavy. They went toward the place where the light was strongest; Toro fell in beside him, his tail wagging and his tongue hanging out.

"You live here?" he asked as she sat him in a comfy chair by a little pot stove built with a pipe that sent the smoke somewhere away. She stuck a bowl of soup in front of him and held out a spoon.

"All my life." She took a seat across from him, petting Toro.

"Alone? How?" He sipped the steaming liquid, savouring the rich, unfamiliar flavour. "What is this?"

"Mushrooms, onions, and other stuff, and, no, Toro's my company." He gaped at her, his brain muddled.

"Oh, boy, don't you stare so. I'm not a demon or anything so scary. You are not hallucinating. I once had a wife and even a mom and dad, but they passed away as did her family."

Teddy sipped his soup, trying to think of what to say. His thoughts wouldn't clear. "I lost my parents too, but others took care of me... oh, oh." He jumped to his feet.

"My Pa, he'll think I'm dead. I need to help him. The ratdogs." His head swirled, and he fell back in his seat.

"You sit, boy, before I need to scoop you up from the floor." She put a hand on his arm. "You're not ready to go dashing off." A look of recognition came over her face. "Oh, you are the boy from above." She wiggled a digit at him. "I remember you and another shorter one and a bigger one, clumsy looking. You were scrounging about the upstairs."

"My Pa," he said weakly, his lungs burning.

"Relax, boy, I'll get to your father. Where'd you leave him?"

"Parking C," he mumbled, his head thicker than a brick wall.

She laid him down on a couch on his side and whacked his back. More water poured out as he started to cough. She stopped and cocked an ear near his chest as though listening to him breathe.

"Lungs are empty. You rest, and I'll be right back."

His head was so heavy. Exhausted, he fell into a dream. He was strolling in a field with the sun shining down and birds flying about, but he did not feel the warmth or hear them sing. Nor did he sense the grass beneath his bare feet. He only knew what they were from the pictures he had seen. He had touched his arm and felt his skin, but the vegetation was nothing to him. All he had was his own self as though he was sealed away from all other forms of life. Terrified, he began to panic, but he heard a laugh he recognized and relaxed. He opened his eyes as the laughter became more present and drew him back to consciousness.

"Pa?" he croaked, his throat aching.

"Ah, my boy," his father exclaimed, his face before him with tears streaming down his cheeks. "I thought I had lost you."

He wrapped his father in a hug. "Oh, Pa. I'm sorry. I slipped and fell in."

"That's okay; that's okay. You're okay, and this is all that counts," Pa said, stroking his head.

Teddy inched his aching body into a more comfortable position, and his father was beside him with a supporting arm. He smiled at the lady across from them before he turned back to his father. "How did you get away from the ratdogs?"

"Oh," his father shrugged as though a bit embarrassed. "I got the first one with my knife and threw my light at the second, and the creature ran. Didn't hurt I yelled my brains out. When I turned around and you were gone, I thought I'd die right there. Spent the next while searching everywhere until Nuna here found me blathering like an idiot."

"Ahg, you weren't so bad." She dismissed his comments and gave him a mug of steaming liquid. "People around here are so far and few between, it is only right we fall apart when we believe we've lost one."

He and his father exchanged glances. "So, there are others?" Pa asked.

Her gaze shifted, and she fidgeted restlessly with her clothes. "There were," she admitted with an uncomfortable laugh. "I suppose somewhere there still are."

"I don't understand."

She slapped her hands on her lap. "Oh, I guess this all deserves a lengthy explanation. Or not, but I haven't had anyone to talk to in," she waved a dismissive hand, "oh, forever. Don't need much of a calendar around here. My people, what there was of them, lived in the ruins that way."

The woman gestured north then pointed further west. "Maybe it was that way. Never been much good at directions. We lived in these passages and the food dwindled as the water ran out. Oh, hell, the whole place slipped down a hole of irretrievable destitution. Pretty soon, there was little left, and my wife and I figured we'd take our family and search for somewhere better. Well, no one wanted to come with us. They all chose to hold on and stay and search the area a little more. They were certain they would hit the grand bucket of resources. We couldn't get them to leave, so we went ourselves."

"That must have been scary."

She shrugged. "It was what it was. Well, we made our way here, and it was a good thing too, 'cause when we went back to tell them about the little oasis we discovered, the passage back had collapsed. So, we made a home here," her voice got hollow as did her gaze, "and that was that."

It might be because his body was mushy like pasty potato bread, but he was having difficulty sorting her story out. "So, your wife is... where?"

His father put a hand on his leg, and he shook his head. "She's no more, my boy, just as so many others."

They fell silent, the weight of their reality pulling them all down as though the air was low in oxygen. Uncomfortable, Teddy let his gaze wander the room.

The place wasn't too awful. Shelves of canned goods lined the walls; as well, she had a small pile of clothing in a basket and some cleaning supplies his mother would drool over. She even had some dishes in decent condition and a painting of an empty field over the table. The most curious item emanated a strange glare from strips anchored to the ceiling. How did she get that? He stood, attracted to the radiance, which seemed like magic. All he wanted was to touch it and check if the light was real.

"I wouldn't if you don't mind," she said, and he froze just as his fingers began to sense the heat from the bulb.

"Oh, sorry, it will burn?"

"I imagine so, but most likely fall out and burst into a million dangerous pieces of airborne shards."

Pa snickered while Teddy sat on his hands. "So, how does it work?" he asked instead.

"Don't know. I'm no so talented with electricity as my wife was. When she saw the flowing water, she built this steam-induced generator to supply power. That's what you almost got sucked into."

"Incredible," exclaimed his father, his eyes the size of Ma's potato-cakes. He jumped to his feet and paced in small circles. "So, you live here, Nuna, and you have electricity, and food, and access to a whole world above you. This is amazing."

Teddy's stomach protested its emptiness.

She took a box from the shelf and gave it to him. Oat and rosemary crackers, he had never had those before. He ripped the top open and dug in, delighting in the new flavour, despite the usual stale aftertaste.

"I suppose," she said. "This is where I do my laundry, though. We never stay here too long; too many of those strange wild dog creatures."

"There's more?" his father said, chuckling euphorically as he took a cracker. "Could we, that is, would you mind if we explored a portion? We don't want to intrude. It's just, well," he blushed a little, "this is exciting, you see."

Nuna waved at him. "Understandable. It's so good to talk to someone again. Now, I told you about me, what brought you here? I'm guessing your story is not too different than mine, but I am hopeful."

"Oh, well yes, about the same," his father began, scratching at his neck.

"Except for the few greedy soul-sucking leeches devouring life and breath of everyone else," Teddy said under his breath.

"I'd like to be kinder than that, but he sums the situation up quite well," Pa agreed. "There are a few people controlling everything people need to stay alive, and they make the rest of us grovel for it."

She stared in surprise. "The few, the many? We came from a gathering of about twenty people. How many of you are there?"

Teddy sunk into the couch; a whole crate of fears opened up inside him and spilled out everywhere. "What difference does it make? They are people needing a new world. They sit in filth and beg for the air they breathe."

"Ted, relax," said his father.

"This may seem like the answers to your searching, but you can't throw..." She paused, her attention taken by something he could not see in the dim space around them. "We should take ourselves elsewhere. It is getting late, and this part is unsafe; the animals see this as a larder because of the water. They come to drink and hunt each other."

Pa helped him to his feet, and they hurried after her as she left the hovel. As she dragged open a rusted door with bits missing out of it like a moth-eaten cardigan, she flicked a switch on the wall, and the lights behind them went out. He stared be- hind him, marveling at what he could only equate to a true expression of a magic he had only ever read about. The hallway they entered had lighted fixtures running down its length, and the glow made him feel exposed. He had dreamt of living in a world without gloominess for so long that when facing the reality, he thought he would feel elation. But he was accustomed to the security of the shadows. Here he was surrounded by luminosity, and he wanted to shrink away and hide.

"Pa, we should get back to the others," he whispered, pulling on his father's sleeve.

"Don't worry, Ted, we'll get back. Your brother and Georges know we may not be back for a day or two."

"But, Pa...."

"Teddy, patience. You've been through a horrible ordeal, and you need rest. For the moment we are safe, and, I'll admit I am more than a trace curious."

Chapter 9

Teddy decided not to argue. He stuffed his hands in his pockets and shuffled on. His head and chest still hurt and he was having wobbly moments as he went. He had to agree, the possibilities of this part of the world appeared limitless, but would she share them—and if she wouldn't, then what?

Nuna hummed as she went ahead of them, her hands clasped behind her back; her ratty sweater hung in drapes of faded colour and ripped threads. She should have been like others living underground—hair tied up in a knotted mess, dirt so deep it coloured the skin, and some physical limitation, a limp or missing digits. However, she was all healthy and clean.

"So, where are we going?" Pa asked. "A collection of stores converted to a home or a series of apartments and you chose the golden one?"

Nuna tilted her head. "A blend of both. I can't say what bits of the past your people carved out for your society, but my wife and I did find what one might consider a paradise. We called the next room the fountain plaza." She paused and opened another door, which led to a stairwell.

They went up and up, and the air became fresher and warmer. Teddy still felt a little unstable, so he was glad when they left the stairs. Despite having a vivid imagination, he was not ready for the spectacle he beheld when they went through the door.

Enormous was an inadequate word; the room would hold a third of Uppercity with ease. Lights of all sorts dangled high above them—stars caught inside, issuing beams, which sparkled and reflected off cool, clear pools of water spilling over each other into a basin wider than his room.

"Of all the beauty," said Pa, his voice faint. He twirled around, his arms extended and his hands outstretched. "This, this is beyond..."

"Words." Teddy leaned against a chair near the side of the fountain, his chest burning and ribs aching. His head was soggy and his breathing difficult.

"This, I believe, they called a hotel in the past. We dubbed the place the tower because the building goes up four floors." Nuna told them with a grin on her face. "We were thrilled when we found it. The water is drinkable and refills via a complex plumbing system. We mapped out the ebbs and flows of the setup. As far as I understand, the water flows to a valve, which pumps it in by some trick of gravity. Any better explanation would take more research than we had time for."

She raised a hand toward row upon row of balconies stretching high above them for four more floors. "Each one of these is a suite with a bed and bath. We spent some time figuring the plumbing out and contrived to get everything working with the assistance of a generator and what remained of the ancient system. Pumps and steam, pipes and gears. My wife was gifted with changing them into conveniences I almost never thought possible. She had a terrible sense of direction, but could make anything out of anything."

"Sounds like you, Pa," Teddy said, poking his father's thigh. "Always turning nothing into something."

"Ahh, that may be true, but I never engineered something like this. I never had such potential to work with."

"I think the boy needs to rest," Nuna said, nodding in Teddy's direction. She placed a hand on his sweaty forehead and lifted his chin, peering in his eyes. "What hurts?"

"Oh, uhh."

"Teddy, you okay?" Pa said, crouching by him. He took his hand. "You hurt, boy? I am so sorry. I was so distracted, so enthralled, I never even thought you might have been injured by your fall."

"I'm fine, Pa, I... my ribs and my lungs... they ache a little, but I think I'm good."

"Come, let's find you a bed and check things out. After, you can rest," said his father, helping him up.

Teddy didn't argue as Pa gathered him up in his arms and gently carried him away. As they went, the lights passed by and blurred, his eyes drooping until he slept.

He woke to the sound of raucous laughter. The bed was so comfortable and did not move, lean, or make him hold on in his sleep for fear of ending up on the floor. He wanted to stay.

Someone laughed again, and the noise grated against his ears, intruding on his dreams.

"Not so loud, Georges. You'll wake the boy."

It was Nuna and Georges. Georges? He was still dreaming.

"Sorry," she said in something more like a grating cry than a whisper. "You are the most interesting person I have had the pleasure of being with in quite, quite some time."

"And you are the most despairing creature I have yet to discover, but I can't say I don't enjoy your company." She barked out her amusement and Nuna shushed her again.

"We're to monitor the boy, not wake him," she scolded. "Now, eat your food and be quiet."

The thought of food sent his stomach into cramps and loud protests of emptiness. He opened his eyes to slits of sunlight filtering through a window to his right. Heavy blankets of red and blue covered him, and the room lacked the usual stink of decay and mould. Georges sat at a table eating something, which smelled so good he salivated.

"Oh, dear, we woke you," Nuna declared, noticing him. "I am so sorry, my boy, but you must be hungry. Here, sit up and munch this."

She sat by him with a full plate in her hand. He wiggled into a better position, which would allow him to eat and breathe with as much comfort as his stiff body would give him.

"Tender?" she said, handing over the food. Her golden dog put a paw on his bed, but she shooed him away.

He stared at his meal. "This isn't dog, is it?" he asked, lifting up a slice. His mouth watered, fearful of what she might offer him. Toro looked at him with sad brown eyes, and his stomach went queasy.

Georges roared and slapped the table.

"Quiet, you," she ordered. "You tell his father he is awake. Go on, leave with your barking laugh and your terrible manners."

"Your wishes, I obey," she told her with grandeur and left with a portion of meat to chew.

Nuna rose from the bed and went to the window, pulling the curtains aside. Sunlight filtered and hurt his eyes.

"Is that safe?" he asked, holding a hand over his face.

She chuckled and ran a hand down Toro's neck. "As safe as the food, boy, which is raccoon, not dog, cat, or even rat. It is only sunshine. The room is sealed. They all are. The only air that comes in or out is the stuff filtered through this massive mechanical device, which grinds and whirs, and my wife tinkered with until we could breathe. She was a genius."

"You must miss her. She sounds like a wonderful person."

A soft smile touched her lips. "She was, and I loved her, but she was too absorbed in what she was creating and got careless."

"That's how she died? Tinkering with her machines?"

Her face lost its tenderness. "Yes, I guess. She was always trying to revamp our resources regardless of how often I told her things were fine the way they were. Luxuries were her way of making things up to me because we only had the two of us. I would get lonely, and she wanted to distract me. I told her it was a brush with melancholy, but she always wanted to give me more." She drew her sweater closer around her and stared out the window. "You're not eating."

"Oh, uhh," he stopped staring and examined his food. Raccoon seemed good, but he wasn't sure. He plucked a piece and sniffed, not bad.

"Oh, child, eat," she ordered with a roll of her eyes. "Raccoon is good. They're vicious when cornered, but resourceful survivors. Not too many of them come around. Now, try the bread too. I mix in strawberries and other goodies I coaxed to grow here. Broccoli works well. You use the plant when it sprouts. I had some barley growing for a while, but the stuff wouldn't go to seed, so that was as far as things got."

While she went on about her gardening, Teddy nibbled on the raccoon. The moment the slice touched his tongue his taste buds came alive as though they had never indulged in food before.

"Oh, this is good," he said, mouth full with juices and succulent meat. He took a bite of the bread and took pleasure in the sweet burst of flavour.

"Don't let Ma hear you say that," Jolon warned as he came in the room and plopped on the bed, snagging a tidbit of raccoon. Nuna smiled at them both and took her tray, leaving them alone. "So, you gonna live?"

"Mmmm. Yes," he answered, swallowing. "My ribs are sore, but my lungs don't hurt anymore."

"Pa told me you went through some kinda septic drainage system and almost got eaten by a steam generator, whatever that is. Did it have teeth?"

Teddy laughed. "It's a machine—makes power. Isn't this place amazing? I thought the mall was mind-blowing, but this... this is incredible."

His brother put his hands behind his head. "Yeah, if you like comfy beds, large rooms, and real running water, but the place lacks stenchy air and filth piles to crawl over."

"And seeping walls..."

"Yeah, that too. Oh, how are we ever going to call this home?" He leaned back on an extra pillow and put his hands behind his head, a self-satisfied expression. "Did you know I got a warm bath today? I guess the lady's wife had built a way to heat the water, and Pa expanded on her idea to include more rooms. Some kinda vast tank warmed by fire. It was so odd to not save the water for someone else. You gotta try a soak. Now he's working to increase the steamy thing, so we get more power."

"How long was I out?" he asked, wondering what he missed.

"Ehh, the night and half the morning. Pa went and got us right after he had tucked you in all sweet and cozy. Georges and I were trying to find a way to make ourselves something more than a cookie sandwich when he dragged us to paradise. Gotta admit, I'm enjoying this."

Shoving back his blankets, Teddy winced his side aching. He sat up and tugged on his pants. "Where is everyone?"

Jolon yawned and gave a half-shrug. "At the tables, I think."

"Tables?" he asked as he got to his feet. His abdominal muscles twitched, and he grimaced.

"It's the room with all the tables. You didn't see that, did you?"

He searched around the room for his shirt and found it shoved under a chair. "Nope, I didn't see much."

"Yeah, those are quite the bruises you got. Uh, I don't think you are allowed to get up."

Teddy drew his top over his abs, hiding the black and blue pattern splattered across his skin. He didn't remember what he hit, but he was surprised he didn't get more of them considering the convoluted torture he went through. "You might try to keep me here, but that would entail putting in some effort." He thwacked his brother's leg. "Come on, lazy, let's check on what's up."

With a reluctant sigh, Jolon rolled off the bed and staggered behind Teddy. "You have no concept of how hard I worked while you were busy sleeping."

His brother led him down a stretch of hall with a yucky ornate carpet of red and green. "Where are we going?" he asked, wondering why anyone would choose such a horrible colour for anything.

"We gotta go down a floor and through the centre court to this kitchen area. It leads to this room called a restaurant where people ate in groups... together... on purpose... seems odd." He waved back toward the room. "Um, you didn't happen to look out the window, did you?"

"No, Jol, I'm not going back to the room."

"When I got up this morning, I stared outside for almost... well, a long time. Made me want to step out and fly or something."

He increased his speed. "Yeah, I gazed out of windows before. All you get is a pile of dirt and stone. The light's amazing, but that's about it."

"Uh, Teddy, you ought to check out the view."

"Later, I want to know what's going on. Now, where's the stairs?" Jiggling handles, he checked door after door.

"End of the hall," Jolon said, a resigned note in his voice. "I tell yah, you're missing something. Come on, they're down a level and a few steps more. You make sure Pa understands I tried."

"Fine," Teddy said and followed his brother. When they arrived at the courtyard, he stopped and stared. Lights sparkled everywhere like dancing angels. The sound of the water played on his ears, gurgling and singing with bliss.

"Heaven on a platter, yeah, yeah, la-di-da. Come on, Ted. Close your mouth and stop staring. You can be a fine interpretation of a stone fish later."

"This is amazing, right?"

"Uh-huh. Didn't you want to see Pa?"

"Yeah."

"Well, let's go."

He left the plaza behind and continued with his brother down a small hall with weird fake plants and pictures of trees and puppies.

"See, tables and chairs... lots of chairs," said Jolon as they went through a double set of potato-brown doors and into a room just as his brother described.

It seemed incredible to him that any society would need a room full of so much furniture. His father, Georges, and Nuna were in the depths of a heated discussion at one of those tables.

"This is impossible," Georges was saying, banging a cup against the table. "You can't expect to hide something like this from the rest of Uppercity."

"I don't give a crap about your Upperlords," Nuna snapped back. "You are talking about bringing, what did you say, about three or four hundred people to this town? How? How?"

"What do you mean, how? We'll parade them through the way we got here."

She began pacing, wringing a towel in her hands. "That's not what I mean. This place may seem like paradise, but supplies are not limitless."

"This place must contain at least a hundred rooms... most of them usable as far as I can tell, with two large beds in most of them. Plus, we have the mall, which can be converted into an endless possibility of homes."

Nuna stared at him as though he had suggested she grow another arm. "Oh, of course, let's stack people everywhere. Our resources are limitless. Oh, wait. Food, where do we find that? Hmm. Well, we'll devour everything, and all die off later. Then again, there's the water. Let's use everything all up, overload the system, and drown in our own excrement."

"Your wife built a tremendous sewage structure..."

"Don't bring her into this."

"Nuna, calm down," Georges said, waving at her with a white scrap of cloth. She pushed aside her plate and sat back in her chair. "These kinds of things can be sorted out. Our greatest concern is how to keep certain Upperlords turning this place into their private club."

"No." She spat and crossed her arms. "No, it is not happening. You people can stay here if you want. The company would be pleasant, and I basically like you all. However, that's it. We either seal the doors so no one else can come through with you all on this side or the other side. Doesn't mean much to me, but if you let any more people in, this place will be lost and then what?"

"But what about the others?"

For a moment, he wished he had kept silent as they all turned to stare at him. His thoughts went to all the wretched Underlings suffering and dying without a chance at any kind of life. "What about Deb and Henri, Caden and Ma? What about Mrs. Fish and her trail of dependents? There are people scraping around like animals in the dirt and rubble trying to find something to keep them going for another moment, and here we have the riches to save them, and we're supposed to pretend nothing is here? Or, better yet, let's stay here and forget about 'em. We'll keep this all to ourselves and forget they exist."

"It's not so simple," Nuna said.

"Oh, hell, who cares about what we can or cannot support? The Upperlords won't let you keep this place to yourselves," Georges roared, leaping to her feet.

"And how are they going to find out?" she demanded, getting in the Upper's personal space.

Georges sputtered and spurted to a stop.

"Georges, you can't tell them," Pa said. He got out of his chair and put a hand on the woman's shoulder. "Georges, this is important. You can't tell them."

She started to chuckle. "Ahh, Tru, I'd love to believe this paradise could happen. I'd love to think we could bring all the Underlings here and set up this terrific little city, which allowed people of every kind to enjoy the sunlight, the grand view through those amazing windows, real beds, and water without limit." "The water isn't without limits," Nuna interjected, but she didn't listen.

"But, Tru, I don't need to tell 'em. There is no way you could evacuate Undercity without them noticing. Those people provide them with a purpose in life. They live off their suffering, and every tiny fragment of scrap underlings dig out. They thrive off their want and need. Life is more than water and food. People need direction. People need a reason to get up in the morning. If Upperlords do not possess power, they will not have a purpose."

"Georges, they are asinine." Pa moved his gaze from one to the other, despair on his face. "We can work this out so every- one can thrive in comfort and protect our resources too."

"You're a dreamer."

"This is ridiculous," Nuna said, shaking her head.

"How?" Teddy asked, looking into her eyes. She turned away, and he shifted to the Upperlord. "Why? Think about what you are saying. You are condemning hundreds of people to their deaths. You gotta understand."

"Ted, you shouldn't be out of bed."

"Come on, boy, we'll get you some water and a book or two. Your father's right. You should be resting," Nuna said, turning him around.

He tried to turn back, but her hands were firm on his shoulder.

"You too," she ordered Jolon. "No one's making any decisions at the moment, so you needn't stress," she added with a pointed glance backward.

They stopped by a desk, and she took out a couple of books from a drawer, which she shoved in his hands. Just days ago, he would have been thrilled with something new to read, but right at that moment, he wanted to throw them at something.

"I don't want a book or anything," he said as she guided him back to his room. "I want you to understand what is happening on the other side of this world."

She opened his door and ushered them in. "Now, we'll talk later. You rest and relax."

"I can't relax," he shouted, but she closed the door and left them alone. "Thanks for the help," he snapped, but his brother gave an indifferent shrug and lay out on the bed across from Teddy's.

"They've been going over the same argument for most of the day. I tried to get my credit's worth in earlier, but they're efficient at shutting down anyone who is too young to deserve an opinion. That's about when I took to staring out windows and taking baths. At least, it felt as though I was doing something. Georges fears the Upperlords are going to hear of this place and take over. Nuna is afraid we'll bring so many people here the resources will run out, and this place will die too, and Pa wants every one of us, Uppers and Underlings, to be happy. Don't know how they're gonna fix this, but I don't want to leave."

He tossed the books on his bed. "What about Ma and Deb, Caden, and Henri? You wanna abandon them on the other side?"

His brother glared at him. "No, that's not what I meant. Don't accuse me of being a selfish ass. It's hard to dismiss some- thing like this once you found it and go back to that hole." He jabbed toward the window. "Look at the view, dopy. It isn't dirt. It's beautiful and amazing, and you're missing it."

Teddy refused. "I don't need any more reasons to stay here."

"Check out this room. Isn't the light different, softer, but more intense? This isn't like gazing out a crack in Uppercity. This is... incredible."

"Incredible, right. Fine." He leaned on the sill and took a peek out the window, and then gaped, holding his breath. He gripped the frame tightly, his fingers turning white. Trees, majestic, tall, sweeping trees stretched out far into the distance, their luscious green leaves dancing in a breeze he longed to feel. "Oh."

"Uh, huh," Jolon said behind him. "How do you leave that?"

"I always imagined what the outside was like, but... it's a forest."

"What's a forest?"

"That is," Teddy replied, pointing to the vast grove of mysterious trees. "At least, that is what my books describe as a forest. I don't know. They might be called weeds, or something else plant-like, but who cares? This is amazing. It doesn't need a name."

"Haven't seen anything moving, though. I searched for most of the morning when the sunlight invaded my sleep, and you refused to get up."

"What do you think you'll find?"

He shrugged in his usual Jolon way. "Can't say. I guess I'm hoping there's something out there alive so we could say—hey, we can live out here—and all this survival scrounging would mean nothing. We could all live... start over... climb a tree." His brother sunk back down on his bed and stared up at the ceiling. "I'm empty. I shouldn't be this tired. Don't you think we're all a little too young, too something to be this worn?"

Teddy sighed, soul-weary. He curled up on his bed. All he wanted to do was find a way to save their people. "Henri would defend this place."

"Huh?"

"I said, Henri, he would fight for this place. So would the others. They would keep it safe. They would do anything to keep the resources from dwindling. They would because they know what life is like in the worst shit hole in existence. I mean, isn't it hard to imagine any place being worse than Undercity?"

"Don't like to dwell on that, but I think you're right. He would defend it, Henri. Not that I think he would be able to with his sad eyes, but he would try. I would try."

"So would I," Teddy admitted.

"Do you think other places like this exist?" his brother asked after a moment.

He thought about this. "Makes sense there would be. Nuna came from somewhere, and we found this place." "Why didn't anyone ever find it before?" Jolon asked as he rolled over and supported himself on his elbows.

"Don't know, but consider how much time it took us to get through to here. I think most people, in the beginning, were trying to struggle through and survive with what they had. I figure the general way of life became more important as society settled, so no one even thought there might be anything beyond our world. Think about how long that door had been in Pa's family as a secret treasure before anyone even bothered to venture deeper. Kinda ridiculous to think this was all waiting a few hours' journey away for all this time."

"Yeah, kinda ridiculous. Hey, you wanna read one of those books she gave you? I could use to think of something else for a while."

"Sure," Teddy agreed, taking up one. He propped himself up with some pillows and got comfortable before he opened the first page.

It was a good story he decided as he stuffed the room with images of elves and trees and magic. The descriptions were rich and the characters fascinating, but after the first chapter Jolon propped himself in a chair so he could stare out the window. Teddy studied him for a while and his brother didn't complain. He hadn't been listening; Teddy suspected he had been in another world for a while. Closing his book, he snagged another seat and joined Jolon, putting his feet on what must have been some heating or cooling system in the past. They sat for quite a while, soaking in the view. There was little to see—only trees moving about in a dance that made him wonder if they were alive. The sky was empty, a desolate blue extending forever.

"Do you think we'll ever be able to go out?" Jolon's voice went quiet as though he was saying something forbidden.

"Can't say, but you would think if the trees are thriving, we could too."

"But we haven't seen any other signs of life. Just trees."

Teddy rose and peered downward to the ground. "Well, and the other green stuff. That, I think, is called grass or some kind of plant." He pointed toward the slope of land stretching away from the building at a sharp angle and jutted far below to the beginning of the tree line. "Seems the first floor is almost completely buried underground, so even if we wanted to get out, we would have to find another way."

"Don't start thinking of how to get out."

They whirled around. Nuna placed a tray of food on a side table and joined them at the window.

"That was the first thing we talked of when we arrived here and saw the view," she said, leaning against the sill. "For days, we would do nothing, but stare out these windows yearning to know what it would feel like. The scene captivates you—pulls you in and you find yourself wishing..." She fell silent, and they waited. "But you don't know what you're longing for." She shoved the tray toward them. "Feed yourselves. Don't get locked up, or your days will go by, and you'll dwindle away."

"Is that what happened to your wife?" The sentence spilled out of him before Teddy could close his mouth.

The look she gave him revealed her pain, and she sank on the bed, her eyes shimmering. "No, to me," she admitted. "I couldn't stop no matter what she tried. I would watch and cry. I don't even know why I cried. Everything hurt so much. Never saw anything more than the trees, but your mind messes about with you, and you start to think you have. I swore I saw someone moving out there once. It was right in front of the open patch. I even showed my wife, but she didn't see anything.

I think that was the day she resolved to try to find out if we could leave the building. I guess she felt it was the only way she could bring me back from the hole I had fallen into. It was a slice of desperation, but I couldn't stop."

"So, what happened?" Jolon asked with a cautious glance to Teddy.

"Don't know, not sure. It is all muddy, a half-melted picture like some of those you find in the rubble. All I know is she was gone, and it took me days and months to crawl out of my hole." She sniffed and wiped her face. "I don't want you people to leave. This place is too large and quiet to live here by myself."

"We can't go back," he said, leaning on her vulnerability. "At least, not to stay. There is no life there. People are scraps of survival. They mean nothing to anyone except for those who can't seem to do anything about it."

"Teddy."

He cut off her protest by placing a hand on hers. "Come with us."

"What?"

"Yes." The thought improved as he thought about it. "Come with us and see for yourself."

"Oh... oh, oh, oh. I don't... no." She stood, brushing him away and skittering about the room like a trapped spider.

"It's a good idea," Jolon added. "Our mom would like to meet you, and you would like her lots."

She jolted to a stop and stared at them with a slicing glare. "I bet you two think you are clever. You have this plan I'll be moved to compassion and, and...."

"And what, dear lady?"

It was Georges standing in the doorway behind Pa.

"Let the hordes descend? That's a side issue. This is an insane thought...."

"Oh, yes, Georges, we all know what you think," his father snapped, his face flicking from complacent to annoyed. "You're a little mouse peeping out from under your covers and sneaking around the edges. The rest of us need more to survive."

"Oh, fine," She pattered off to the window. "Don't listen to me. The brute I gave you is no match for the squad you'll have upon you when the Upperlords cling together, but what does that matter? What do I know? I'm a mouse... eep, eeep, eep."

Teddy laughed. It hurt, but he couldn't stop, and it spread through to the others like a cold.

"Fine, fine," Nuna gasped as the fit dwindled to the odd twitter. "I'll come, I'll see, but I make no promises."

Pa bowed and winked. "That's more than I hoped for.

Chapter 10

"Well, this is... is... well... it is good to meet you," Ma stammered as she stood with her hands full of old dresses she had been trying to mend.

Mrs. Fish didn't rely on ceremony or manners as she paced around Nuna like a bug looking for a place to land, chuckling and clicking her tongue. "A new person. My, my." She lifted a corner of Nuna's coat. "Plus, she's clean, sparkling clean."

"Fish," Ma scolded as she dumped her load on a nearby box and opened her arms. "Come now, Nuna, let's leave the ware- house. It's a claustrophobic place. Our home is over here, and I just put a pot of water on. We don't carry much for tea, but Henri found a few leaves the other day."

She gestured to the brute standing by Caden—not too near to annoy her, but close enough to be attentive.

"Hey, scroungers, it's about time you showed up," Caden greeted, falling in behind them as they went to the house.

Henri doted along, happy to be with her. While he cared for his sister, Teddy didn't understand the attraction. He guessed they balanced each other out, her aggressive cynicism and his soft mushiness.

"Good to see you too," Jolon said.

Their parents, Mrs. Fish, Georges, and Nuna gathered around the table in a huddle, which left no room for anyone else. Teddy stopped, and they piled into him.

Caden shoved him. "Give warning."

"I'm done with this," he muttered, not wanting to hear any more of the adult conversations he was not able to be a part of. "I'm going to my office. If you guys want to come, fine, but they're going to sort out their territory whether we say anything or not. I'd rather wait for the outcome somewhere else."

They trailed behind as he ascended the stairs. He halted at the place where they used to climb the rail to get over to the landing. A crude, narrow bridge now spanned the distance.

"Surprise," Caden said with a smidgen of enthusiasm. "Henri built it." She punched the brute on the shoulder. "Didn't ya, brawny?"

He glowed red and grinned. "Easy."

For him, Teddy decided as he took a step onto the metal surface stretching across the space between the stairs and the landing. Well, it was solid. He crossed over and went into his office, making himself comfortable in his chair.

"So, what like? Is good?" Henri asked, sitting on the floor in front of him.

"Better than that," Jolon said, perching on a stool by the window.

"We live there?" he asked. "Healthy?" He snuck a glance at Caden as he said this, the hope in his eyes vivid.

"That's the plan, I guess...I don't know," Teddy answered, thinking about Nuna. "The place has running water and power, and rooms, beds, air. I don't think the Uppercity can even compare. There's room and sunlight. You can see through the windows..."

He glanced Jolon's way. His brother kept his attention on the main floor; his face dejected as though he didn't like the view.

"Trees stretch out beyond any distance I ever thought possible," Teddy added, dejected by how dingy and empty the warehouse had become.

"So, what's the problem?" Caden asked. "The lady?"

Teddy picked up a broach he kept to fix for his mother. "Look at this thing. I found it in a jumble of rubbish after my parents disappeared. I replaced a couple of the jewels, but the hinges are bent, and the clasp doesn't want to stay closed. Doubt I'll ever get it right."

"Nuna's a difficulty, yes. She's been living there for quite a while, first with her wife and after by herself. There's no one else, but she's afraid if we bring everyone from Undercity there, we'll drain the resources and end up worse than we are now."

"But can't stop us? Not if just her?" Henri said, coming closer.

"No, I guess not, but Pa feels it wouldn't be right not to consider her feelings. She was there first. She's willing to let us," he gestured at them, "stay, but as to anyone else? I can't tell you."

"So, we get paradise, and everyone else can live in hell?" Caden scoffed, sinking lower in her chair.

"That's not the only problem," Teddy continued. "Georges is afraid the Uppers will move in if they find out."

"She better not tell." The tone in the brute's voice was unsettling. "They got paradise." "She thinks they'll all die if the Underlings go."

Jolon's chuckle was bitter. "She's right. Though, I don't know if they deserve to survive."

"Eh, they'll live," Caden said. "They'll get a coating of dirt, but they'll live."

"Still, we would need to get everyone out without them finding out. That'll be quite the tricky manoeuvre," said Teddy.

"Yeah, I figure Georges won't even need to tell them once their slaves start disappearing," Jolon added.

"It's all pointless if Nuna won't agree to the move," Teddy said with a sigh.

Henri thrust his bulk to his feet, his face set like a brick. "She no say. She no say. She only one, and we many. She can't turn away, if does then doesn't deserve paradise."

"So, what do you suggest we do? Toss her in a pit?" he asked, not liking where the brute's anger was headed. "No," he said, pulling himself back. "We can't have all, and refuse to let anyone in, can we?"

"I don't know if it's that easy."

He stalked back and forth, his bulk shaking the room. "So we get mess while all else blah? No."

"Calm down, brute," Jolon said, putting out a hand.

"I not brute," he insisted, pulling his hair back. "I not. People think I am because I big. I didn't choose. I am. Like all we are." He left them, and they sat in silence for a while.

"He is strange," Caden said in a low grumble. "Brings me a different flower every day—some real, some not. Don't know where he gets 'em, but he shows up with a flower every day."

The idea made Teddy smile. He gave a half-hearted laugh. "I guess we all are strange."

"He's right, though," Jolon said, taking a seat. "We can't do nothing, despite what Nuna or anyone else wants." He fingered a plastic lamp piece and twirled it. "We're surrounded by junk and pretending it's fantastic."

"No one's pretending," Teddy threw the broach aside. Maybe it was all trash. "So, what do we do? Voice our protest? Demand change? Done. Done a few times if you think of the last few days. We wanted to improve things, and now we are waiting on the fringe of growth, and we have no clue how to step over. It seems simple. It's right in front of us. All we need to do is cross over the line. Do we? No. We stare and say, 'wouldn't that be wonderful.'"

"Oh, shyza. Shut up. I've had enough whimpering," Caden said, rubbing her forehead with her hand. "Let's go back and face them. Henri spits out strings of rants about the state of the world, and you simper about how powerless we are. This is all so annoying. We'll find out what the adults want to do and, after, we'll decide what we want to do. This is all rubble and crap otherwise."

"Why not," Teddy said, getting to his feet. He rushed after her with Jolon right behind them. "And I don't simper."

"Right," his brother and sister said together.

When they reached the kitchen, the others were still at the table, but now it was set for dinner.

"Food's waiting," Ma said, and they sat down to fried potatoes and bits of scraggly carrots.

After tasting Nuna's cooking, Teddy disliked potatoes. He reminded himself not to be so self-centered.

"I guess we could slip people out a few at a time." Georges conceded as she flickered her fork about.

"I thought you didn't want anyone to relocate to the tower," he said.

"Not quite true. I'm concerned with the consequences of moving. I'm a chicken like your father said," she said with more pride than chickens appeared to possess. "Besides, now that we're back," She hiccupped and held up her fork with a potato on it. "I don't want to stay. Done with potatoes. No disrespect, Tisha, they're good. Just bored with them."

Nuna tugged her coat around her and gazed at what Teddy used to think of as a pleasant home. Her face was pale and slack as though defeated and she had nothing left inside.

"And this is a good home," Ma said with a sigh.

Mrs. Fish bobbed her head and cackled. "This is, this is, but I always wanted a little, well, less rubble in my life." She stood by Nuna, her countenance hopeful and sceptical. "So there may be enough room for my brood?" She jerked a thumb at the cluster of children clambering about with Deb leading them. Most of them were more orphans she had taken in like his parents had done. They were all strays of Undercity, broken, in pieces, but pretending all was well, smiling and laughing as though there were streaks of sunshine everywhere.

Nuna stared with her lip quivering and her hands clenched. She tightened her jaw and said, "Fine. Fine. I suppose there is room for everyone. Doesn't matter what the future might hold. Can't let the present keep going on like this."

"Well, there's only the issue of figuring out the how," Pa said. Georges went to speak, but an alarm rang, and Teddy's father stood. "We've got customers. Guess business must go on for now until we get things all sorted out. Come on, Henri. Let's see who's here."

Teddy went along with Jolon and Caden. They crawled up on a few crates to get a better view without being seen. It was Belinda with three brutes and a shorter man missing an eye.

"Well. Truman, you're here in person," Belinda said, giving Pa a raking dismissal. "Good. Have you seen my sister? I checked all her haunts and holes she slips into for days at a time, but haven't been able to find her. This place is about the last dump left to search."

"Your concern is quite poignant, Lindy," Georges drawled as she stumbled in behind Teddy's father and held herself up by a tall statue of a girl missing her head.

"She's drunk?" Jolon asked, whispering in his ear.

"Don't think so. If she is, I don't know what she's been drinking. Ma doesn't let any alcohol in the house."

"She's pretending," whispered Caden on his other side.

"I missed you, too," Georges drawled. "I missed you at the Drunken Nut and Madame Torvel's and the Crooked Curve, and I almost didn't miss you at the Creative Kittens, but this little blondie caught my attention, and I slipped away."

Belinda shook her head. "You are so pathetic. I'm tiring of digging you out from your messes. Coming here to...."

"Oh, don't be so wired, Lindy. I wandered down here looking for some of those charming little boxes Tru had last week. Got a few loves in need of some tokens of affection."

"Ah, and is that where your late night raid of our food supplies went?" Her sister gave a sly laugh and raised an eyebrow. "You think I didn't notice? I hope it didn't go to the rabble."

"You need the rabble, Lindy, you and me and the whole of Upper. We need 'em," she said with a nonchalant slouch as she propped herself on a crate. "Yep, it's a fact. We neglect them, and we lose our world."

Belinda shifted about as though she was trying to avoid what her sister was saying. "There're more of them down here than we'll ever run out of." She made a derisive gesture toward Mrs. Fish's crowd of children who gathered by the door. "They breed and breed, making more pathetic rats over and over. So we lose a few, more will pop up."

"And we're to keep 'em in their place, eh?"

Belinda flicked her gaze around the room and backed up a step closer to her guards. The guy with the patch over his eye stepped forward with his chin held high.

"If we didn't, they would take over and use up all the resources. They don't know any better."

Georges stared at him as though he was something seeping from a bag of garbage. "That is quite a judgment to pass."

"Well, look at them." Belinda swept her hand around the room. "They have no restraint. Left to their own, they would eat everything with no regard for the future." She flipped a finger Jolon's way. "He eats more than his share and where does that leave the others?"

Putting a restraining hand on Pa's arm, Georges laughed. "I wouldn't go on too much about eating more than your chunk, Lindy." She poked her sister in her broad stomach. "We're both a bit free with our piece of things, aren't we? Oh, my, we're all getting far too serious for my amusement to continue. I haven't got an interest in all things Under despite how things might appear to you, so you needn't worry." Patting her sister's cheek, she belched. As she swayed on her feet, she let her face crumble. "I'm feeling rather sober now, so I think it's time I went. Deliver those boxes later, would you, Tru? There are lovelies waiting."

She wagged a finger in Pa's direction and careened her way toward the exit, whistling as she went.

"Is there something you want?" Pa managed with a cold tilt to his grin.

Belinda didn't say anything; she just waited as though frozen, her bitty eyes staring pins into her surroundings.

Pa inclined his head toward Belinda. "My lord? I possess some beautiful pillows my boys found on our last excursion. Would you like to see them?"

"Where do you go?" Her gaze narrowed with suspicion.

"Go?"

"Yes, where do you go on your 'excursions'?"

He spread his dirt stained hands wide. "We scrounge the tunnels. There are several attached to my little hovel here. They don't go anywhere. We sift through them until we find little pockets of goods, or crates and boxes. It's a careful job as you can imagine, but we don't care. As you say, we'd be lost without our purpose. Can't think what we'd do otherwise. I can take you scrounging if you like, but it's dangerous if you don't mind your step. We've had some leakage and snakes this morning, but a flash of fire and they'll clear out. Good eating, if we can trap 'em."

The Upperlord's lip curled at the corner. "That won't be necessary."

"The pillows, my lord? You might fine them quite beautiful."

Teddy climbed down from his perch and left his father to sort out Georges' sister. The woman made him feel worse than his trip through the sewer had.

"Everything all right?" his mother asked as joined her at the table. She brushed his hair with her fingers and touched his cheek. "They told me of your accident, my love, are you still hurting?"

Tears curled down to his chin, and she wiped them. "I'm good... no. I think... I don't know. It's all so tiring."

"I understand, my sweet," she said with a deep embrace. "I understand."

"She's so cold and pompous. She thinks we can't provide for ourselves when they take everything and hoard it. What an excuse."

"Okay, okay."

"But we can. We can," he insisted, slipping out of his mother's grasp and turning toward Nuna. "You understand why we can't stay here? Did you hear her? Did you see her? We can't live here. We're nothing to them."

"Teddy, stop," his mother said. "You're upset. You need sleep. We all do."

Nuna took his hand and rubbed his palm. "We'll do our best, child. I promise. We'll do our best."

Ma hugged him from behind. "Come, now. If we're going to improve our world, we all will need rest. There is much work to do and no one must suspect anything."

"Yes, good advice," Pa said upon entering the room. He kissed his wife and handed her two fat chickens. "I sold your pillows, the silky ones you put together last week and got us some chicken. How's that for a good deal?"

She took the birds and smiled. "You are my hero, as usual, my love."

"Now," he said, rubbing his hands. "Nuna, is there any point in bringing anything with us? As far as I can tell, your world seems pretty complete, but you never know."

"Not that I can see," she said, picking up a potato from the stack by the sink. "Some of these might be good. They seem to be quite a versatile crumb of food."

"Oh, not potatoes," Jolon groaned. "And here I thought we would leave the worst of this place behind."

"Potatoes are a good resource, dear," Ma scolded, holding one under his nose. "You are alive because of potatoes. They grow almost anywhere and make almost anything, so don't scorn your livelihood."

"Ah, Ma, you know I'm joking. I love, love, love your potatoes, your potatocakes, your potato pies, potato chips, and potato soup. I just kinda like to think a little variety would be yummy."

"I'll give you yummy, my sweet. You'll be tending these potatoes once we get a garden going, so learn to love 'em all again."

"Pa, what about Georges?" Teddy asked.

"We'll see her tomorrow. Never fear, my boy. She's not as scattered or careless as she may seem. She wants a different reality as much as we do."

"How?" Henri asked, filling the doorway with his bulk.

"What do you mean? What has got you worried?" Teddy's father asked, turning to the brute.

"All?" he said. "Underling servants. We save?"

"It's a good question. I think we will start first thing in the morning, bringing those we're closest to and trust the most through. Mrs. Fish, you get your brood to help gather those who require assistance and get them moving. We'll need a couple of carts."

"Won't that be noticed?" Jolon asked.

"Not if we pass the word we're having a nursing day to aid those who are in greatest need after the cave-in. We have had 'em before so it won't make too many people suspicious. Get them going through slow and quiet, and we'll build from there." As he finished, they all started tossing in their concerns at once, but he put up his hand.

"Hey, it has been an adventure of a day, and we're all more than a tad done in. We'll talk with Georges tomorrow and work out a system. It may take some time, but we'll get it all planned." He took Teddy by the shoulders and gave him a gentle shove toward his room. "Get some sleep."

He stumbled off to his room and Henri along went with him. The brute dumped himself on his bed and stared at the ceiling tiles. Climbing gingerly into his bed, Teddy left him to his thoughts. There was enough swirling around in his brain to keep him awake for hours yet.

Belinda was a disease. She was a horrible, merciless infection eating away every sign of life. It didn't matter to him anymore what happened to Uppercity. They were a soulless cancer devouring everyone else. They deserved what they got.

Chapter 11

In the early morning, they left home and went to the hand cranked lifts, which brought them to Upper. Pa almost forgot the boxes, and they had to go back again to retrieve them. Teddy went too to carry them, and Henri went along as the closest thing to protection they could come up with. Their brute traded yawns with him as they stepped on the wooden platform and jostled for a position among the Underlings and merchandise destined for Uppercity.

This was a normal day, he reminded himself as paranoia set in, and he began to think everyone suspected what they were about. Every expression, every glance made him fear discovery though he told himself he was being silly.

"Calm yourself," Pa whispered as the platform rose with every pull of the supporting ropes. "This is just another day."

Teddy adjusted his load of boxes as though they were all the worries he had. They left the loading zone behind and went through the crowded market. Everything seemed different despite how static it appeared.

"Pa, I think we're being followed," he asked, his voice hushed as he glimpsed a couple of brutes he thought he had seen with Belinda slip in behind them.

"Uh, yes, I do believe we are," his father said with a cheerful grin and a wave to some other merchant. "I'd say Belinda is a half smidgen insecure and a whole bit demented. Don't worry though. Act normal. We're only making a delivery." Taking a deep breath, he turned to Henri, and the brute frowned at him, his head whirling about as he tried to fulfill his role as their protector.

"Ah, Tru," Georges exclaimed, coming up beside them. She slung an arm around Pa and leaned on him. "You are ever the perfect scrounger. You found my little trinkets?"

Taking note of Teddy's load, she roared. "Oooh, so you did. Delightful. I got a few visitors to... visit tonight, and I promised eternal treasure, well, at least, I promised a box or two. These will grant me favor, tremendous favor. If you weren't so happy in your bliss, I'd almost feel generous and grateful enough to share a portion. Interested? No? Too bad. Now, let's go to my place and settle matters. You must join me, at least, for a drink. I'm bored with my usual company and need fresh conversation."

"Of course, of course, Georges. I would be most pleased to spend some time taking advantage of your stores. I could use something stronger to perk me up today."

The Upperlord shoved on the door to her private chambers and went in with a flourish. As Teddy entered, he glanced back and caught sight of two brutes waiting at the end of the alley.

"Come on, boy. And don't drop my gifts," Georges ordered, and she slammed the door behind them.

"Breath easy, I sent my hag on an errand, which will take her time to fulfill. My sister's spy, she is. Can't trust anyone these days. She is the one who told her about the food. Not good."

She lounged on her couch and motioned for them to sit. "Toss those things, boy," she ordered, meaning the boxes.

Teddy dumped them on the floor with a clatter. "Sorry."

"Whatever." She sighed and turned her attention to his father. "Well, now we've sunk ourselves into a pit. I am guessing you took note of your new shadows? A few Underlings are watching over you too. I hope you feel well protected. I sure do. No matter where I go, my dear sister's creepers go too. How lovely."

"All the more reason to leave," Pa said.

"Oh, for all that is worth saving, please, Tru, don't pretend to think you can go on with this plan. I am all for leaving this place behind too, but how? Sneaking out of hell cannot bring one to paradise. The devils won't allow it." "We have few other alternatives, Georges, you know this. Can you tell me you can forget paradise? Can you leave all the comfort and space behind for this?" He swept a hand over the broken down surroundings and the slit of a window letting in a remnant of light. "You gazed out better windows and discovered a richer world. How can we stay here knowing what exists a few hours away?"

The Upperlord worked her jaw as though she was trying to swallow what Pa told her. "Oh, fine. Might as well go through with this insanity. If all works as hoped for, we find rapture, if not, well, nothing will change except maybe our suffering."

"What mean?" Henri asked, leaning his bulk against the door.

"What do I mean, brute? What do I mean?" She emphasized each word. "I mean if we are discovered trying to leave this dump, they will not only take paradise from us but use us as an example of traitors. First, we'll suffer and after, we'll die. You must remember the group of Underlings who tried to get together last year and take over the power station. I do believe if you go to the South Side pits you can still see what's left of their bodies dangling from ropes over the sewage gardens."

Teddy turned his attention to Pa. He hadn't heard of this. "Your mother and I decided this was information you and your siblings did not need," he explained. "There are things not worth talking about. Their plan was ill-conceived, and they had nowhere to go except here."

"So, what do we do?" Teddy asked, unsettled by the news.

"We seal off Uppercity," Henri told them, his voice low and rumbling. "We cut off, so can't follow. Destroy bridge between here and warehouse. Barricade tunnel to mall. They never find, ever."

Georges raised a disparaging eyebrow. "Doesn't ask for much, this brute of yours, does he?"

"No, but he has a point," Pa said. "He has a good scheme, but how do we flesh the idea out? As you said, there are Upperlords like your sister who own faithful subjects both here and below. We must gather our allies in secret if we are to succeed."

Henri jumped and stumbled on a rusted table leg as a heavy pounding at the door interrupted them. Georges grabbed a decanter and sloshed some alcohol into a glass, thrusting the drink at Pa.

"Oh, for all that is shiny stop your hammering and come in," she ordered, taking a tremendous sip from the bottle.

The brute unlocked the door; his face twisted up in an attempt to appear intimidating. Belinda entered with a few other Uppers and a multitude of brawn-flexing, sullen brutes. The stubby, hairy creeper from the Adult Quarter with Dorkas came in with them. He sneered at Teddy, picking at his teeth and gawking like he had discovered something special.

"Well, what coziness this is," Belinda cooed as she slithered around the room. "Your choice of constant companionship is becoming worrisome, sister."

Teddy scooted back to where Henri stood, noting the stretch of pipe the brute hid behind his leg.

"Eh, you worry too much, Lindy," Georges said with a grunt and a dismissive wave.

"Don't call me that."

Georges belched. "Sorry. Habit. Tru here is as harmless as kittens... or potato pie... or, or...." She belched again, a disgusting breeeeaaak, and Teddy marveled at her prowess. "'Scuse, this bottle contains more kick and bite than he does."

"You're pathetic, Georges. Why do I bother with you? That's enough of your sneaking and debauchery. You are up to something. You think I buy your drunken stupor? You forget I grew up with you and you still think me a sucker. I understand you better than you know yourself. The drunker you appear, the soberer you are. The more the fool you act, the more cunning your intentions." She stepped close, taking the bottle from Georges' hands and pouring its contents to the floor. "What are you up to?"

Georges managed to sit up, wobbling on the corner of the threadbare couch. "I resent those accusations, sister. What do you think anyone can do, conniving or not, in this pitiful shot glass of a world?" She slid down and ended up half under the coffee table. "Limping tunnel snakes, Bel... Bal... Lindy. How can you question my drunkenness? I'm insulted."

"I think maybe we should go," Pa said, teetering to his feet and putting a hand on the end table to steady himself. "I'm afraid your wine is messing with my head a trace too, and I can see this is a family af... affair. Don't want to interfere, so I'll take my child and go."

"And your brute?"

He paused in his steps and half-turned back. "In truth, he's more of a heavy lifting machine. My bones are getting old, and the boys are not growing up fast enough to deal with the balance of our work."

"Yes, Belinda. You said yourself he makes a lousy brute, so I got what I could out of him." Georges thrust herself to her feet, leaning on a heavy cane she fished out from under the couch.

"This is what has you all concerned and tied up?" She laughed. "Here, I make us a deal on a dud, and you get all worried I'm taking over the world. Do you believe I'm that ambitious?"

"Georges, I tend not to think much of you at all. However...." She strolled over to Pa and scanned Teddy from top to bottom, the look in her eyes disturbing. "I have a business proposition for you."

"I suspect I may not like your proposition," Pa said.

Teddy slid in behind Henri. The Upperlord was making him feel turned inside out and he wanted to get away from her. She was so serious without any flicker of emotion.

"Truman, you understand this world has needs, which go beyond the basics of food and pillows. You possess a certain couple of commodities, which would serve well. The Nest is gone, and good stock is low, so prices are high. Now, I realize your daughter is your real child and so your affections for her probably won't allow you to bargain with her; however, the boy is a spare you dug up, as I understand. He is a bit skittish, I'll admit—they tend to be at that age, but his form is good, and he is considered attractive to some. I must tell you I possess two fine offers waiting for his person."

Bile rushed up Teddy's throat and threatened to spill out his mouth. He swallowed many times, his heart pounding.

"This could be the break you wanted," she went on with a slick smile. "You're not like the other Underlings mucking away in the pits. You have potential, uses, and I possess the means to make you and your... family quite comfortable. Think on this, Truman—safety and a new home for your wife and children, a good life for many at the cost of one. There may even be room for you to bring in a few more... orphans." She cast an eye over Teddy. "Even he would get a better life. Happiness for everyone."

She waited, gazing at Pa as though they had been talking about pillows again. In an instant, a myriad of colours shifted over his father's face—a live experience of a morphing Teddy read about in a torn picture book. His father settled on a tight smirk, which hid a clenched jaw.

"Thank you for the honor of your request, but I am afraid I am as attached to my son as I am to my daughter. I must decline your offer and end the day. Georges, thank you for your wine, Belinda..." He worked his stubbled jaw as if trying to let the right words come out. "Another time."

Still holding his pipe, Henri put a hand on Teddy and went to guide him out of the room with Pa right behind them, but the guards at the door stepped in front of them.

"Ah, Belinda, why don't we leave this for now?" Georges suggested, sidling up to her sister, but she dismissed her with a flick of her fingers.

"No, I'm afraid we can't do that. You see, the request was a formality. I am not interested in your personal feelings in this venture. I believe I have been fair in allowing you to keep your daughter, but the boy is a commodity I cannot lose. Therefore, he will stay here, and you will take my offer."

"Like hell!" Pa said and hit Belinda in the head with the wine bottle.

Henri jabbed one brute in his bulging stomach and went to strike the other, but the goon grabbed the pipe and caught him with a right hook. Georges stepped over the coffee table and smashed a statue on the nearest brute.

The creeper snatched at Teddy's arm. "You're mine, pretty boy. Mine."

Teddy kicked at him and punched him in the face. "Get off," he yelled, hitting him again. The creeper fell back, and Teddy gave him another kick before his father grabbed him, hauling him out the door.

They ran down the alley, though two more guards who stood at the end. One tried to catch him, so he ducked under the brute's arms and scrambled under his legs. His father dodged a hit and slashed at the other guy with the remains of the bottle, cutting deep gashes across the man's face. He yowled and brought his hands to his face as Henri rushed up with Georges behind him and took out a piece of brawn with his pipe.

"Guess going in secret is out," she gasped as they ran. "This is going to be hard on my reputation."

"Get to the lifts," Pa shouted as several more guards chased after them.

The foursome weaved through the marketplace turning tables and scattering merchandise as they went. They created chaos as people scrambled everywhere, grasping for goods and trying to protect their livelihood. If it hadn't been for the guys still after them, Teddy would have stopped to laugh at the desperate want driving the Uppers to steal from each other.

As they reached the lifts, sentries stepped forward to catch them, but Henri roared like a true brute and charged. One doubled back and fell against the wooden barrier protecting people from falling down the hole, which allowed the lifts to rise and lower. Henri barged through two goons and threw a red-faced, shouting Upperlord into a brute's chest.

Pa took hold of Teddy, and they jumped on the lift with Georges. Henri yanked on the brake and jumped on as they descended at an uncontrolled rate. Down below, people scattered and they hit the ground hard, sending dust everywhere. Teddy fell down, his teeth rattling in his head.

"Cut the lines! Cut the rotten lines!" Georges shouted, hacking at the ropes, which worked the lifts.

The lift started to rise as the brutes above hauled on the cordage. Henri roared again. He seized a mess of cables and tore them out of their gears, sending bolts and wood everywhere. The whole thing lurched and tilted while Underlings scrambled in panic.

"That'll work," Georges said, and she pushed them forward with more energy than Teddy suspected the woman of having.

"Let's get going. They won't stay up there forever."

They tore through the crowd until they came to the bridge to their home. A line of people blocked their way as they filed into the warehouse. He didn't know what his mother and Mrs. Fish told people, but whatever they said worked and the Underlings scrambled into action. The problem was, they didn't have much time. Teddy and his father weaved their way home while Henri hauled old man Fudge to his shoulder and carried him off, the Underling squealing all the way with his sisters shouting behind them.

"We must hurry this up, Tisha," Pa said, rushing up to their mother. "Time's up."

"H... how can we? There is no way we can get them all in. There's too many of them."

"Get them across the bridge. That'll give us time," Georges suggested as she rested against a crate, holding her side. "Ahhh, haven't expended so much energy since... ever."

"Henri, get a couple of Mrs. Fish's boys and collect those who can't walk well. Haul them in here on carts if you must. Teddy, you and Jolon get up on the balcony and scout for trouble. We've got to get as many as we can across," ordered Pa.

They scooted out the exit and on the walkway, which made a platform overlooking the cavern dividing their home from the rest of the Undercity. The structure wasn't too wide—maybe two feet—but they had a fence they had fashioned out of beams and pipes to keep anyone from falling off. Still, Teddy found himself getting dizzy as he inched along to get to the ladder to the lookout—a smaller balcony they could sit on with poles and ropes to hold to keep them from tumbling into an endless crevice. It took every fragment of concentration on a good day for him to make his way up the bits of wood his father's father had nailed to the side of the building's outer wall to make the ladder. He understood they were sturdy, but there was little else to hold on to. He inched his way over the edge and sat up, slipping a leg around one of the metal poles to give him something stable to secure to. He clutched the ropes strung between the pipes while Jolon crawled in beside him.

"I hate this place," he gasped and locked himself to a pole. "Makes me want to throw up."

Teddy made the mistake of leaning forward and looking down into the endless depth of blackness below him. He shut his eyes and swallowed, clenching the ropes tighter until his hands hurt. "I know," he muttered. "But they're disgusting. Contemptible."

"Who are?"

"Those Upperlords."

"I'm guessing things didn't go well?"

"Nope. Plan fell apart when Belinda showed up." "Hate her. So, she figured things out, or what?" Teddy clenched his teeth; he didn't want to say.

"Well?" Jolon leaned in, flicking Teddy's collar and poking his cheek. "Give up, Ted. What happened?"

He twisted away, catching himself as he sensed he was nearing the edge. "We gotta keep an eye out for Upperlords," he reminded his brother as he scanned the crowd below. Nothing yet, but they still had so many people to bring over. Too many were confused as to what was going on, and they milled about, wandering back and forth. Someone started shouting Uppercity was collapsing, which sent a tear of panic through everyone. Henri jumped in, using his bulk to sort people out and keep the line moving.

"He was amazing," Teddy said, watching the brute. "It was like he tapped into some giant centaur-like the stories and went berserk. He bowled through people like you bowl through food."

His brother didn't appreciate the cut. "What humor, what wit. Now tell me what happened."

"They wanted Pa to sell me."

Jolon choked. "What? You're kidding."

"Nope, and when he said no Belinda said he had no choice, so we bolted."

"Son of a cretin. Son of a slimy, oozing fungus." He swore with what few filthy words he had in his vocabulary. "That sucks."

"Makes me want to trade my skin for something cleaner. They're a sick bunch. I used to feel guilty about leaving them out of the move, but now I don't give a crumb if they get locked in here." He straightened a little as torches appeared in the distance. "They're coming. They're coming!" he shouted, pointing. "Hit the signal, Jol."

His brother scrounged around and dug up one of the flares they left up there for emergencies. He flicked a match and lit it. The string sparked and jumped, throwing fragments of light everywhere. Jolon yelped and let go as the flare shot off fiery bits, which tumbled end over end into the black of the cavern. Those below them screeched and screamed, the remaining crowd pushing their way forward.

Henri grabbed two people at a time and threw them across. After, he stood at the base of the bridge with a shaft of pipe in hand while the rest got to safety. Most people didn't even understand why they were trying to escape. They trailed along like mindless drones, babbling about impending doom. When the other side cleared, Henri shut the metal gate and locked it, sealing both sides with a fence of barbed wire and broken glass.

"Teddy, Jolon, come down," their father called from below. He stood beside their brute near the entrance to the warehouse.

They scrambled down, relieved to be on more solid ground as they snuck in by Henri and Pa.

"Get in, boys," his father said, and they skittered in, hiding right inside the doors to get a clear view. Georges stood with them, watching too.

"You seem well equipped for invasion," she said, impressed.

"Our family learned in the beginning how important it was to guard themselves. The bridge is wired too. No idea if the explosives are any good, but we can try." He tossed a lighter at Henri. "Here, this one still contains some fluid. I kept it for just a situation as this. You see the fragment of string dangling by the edge? It's a fuse. If we must, light it."

The brute caught the lighter and agreed.

"You flick the little wheel," Georges told him as Henri contemplated the little tube, his eyes bugging with confusion.

"Don't try to come any farther," Pa warned while a contingent of Underlords and brutes rushed up the other side. The dogs charged teeth bared and their enemies halted on the other side of the gate.

Belinda stepped forward and touched the barbed wire, but jerked her hand back. "Interesting defenses, Truman. Should have realized you would keep the best for yourselves. We should have monitored you traitors years ago."

"Too late, Lindy," he said, and Georges laughed. "My father never trusted your father and his father never came close to trusting your grandfather, so you didn't expect me to trust you, did you?"

"I suppose not, but what now? We still have some of your Underlings." She motioned to the brutes behind her, and they hauled forth two ragged men Pa worked with before.

"We can't leave them," Teddy's mother whispered as she came up behind them.

"We might not get a choice," he whispered back. "At least for now. With no bridge, we buy some time. We don't need to go to the tower until we figure out a way to get everyone.

"Can't let she believe won," Henri said.

Georges stepped up. "We can. If she thinks we're trapped here. If she believes we possess nothing to live on, she will leave us alone until we surrender—until we come begging for forgiveness and food. We hold the edge, but she doesn't realize this. When she relaxes, we can sneak in and get those people we left.

In the meantime, we can filter people through to the tower in a more orderly fashion and pretend we're all still stored here in your warehouse."

"Not a bad plan," Ma said with an approving frown and Georges nodded in surprise.

"Thanks, Tisha. I never thought I'd hear you like me."

She rolled her eyes at the Upperlord. "I didn't say I liked you; I like your plan."

"Close enough."

"Sorry, Belinda," Pa yelled across the divide. "I'm afraid you must do better than threaten. Consider this a strike and we're holding out until some improvements are made. You and your kind have gone too far, and we're done with being your slaves. You have no right."

She hooted. "No right? Let's see how you all do with no water, no air, and no food. That's your reality, Truman, if you blow this bridge, first the food then the water, and then the air. You get a day to decide before we start shutting things off."

"If they give us a couple of days, we won't need to destroy the bridge," Jolon said.

"I doubt that is their intention," Georges muttered.

"Someone doesn't want to wait." Henri gestured to a band of brutes lugging a thick support beam over to the gate. Belinda and her subjects moved aside and signalled for them to go ahead.

They pulled back a ways and charged, hollering as they went, their voices bouncing around the chamber. Teddy covered his ears as they struck the gate and the sound of the impact reverberated through his skull. Still, the barrier held, so they hit it again and again. On the third pass, the metal creaked and groaned, the hinges bending. Pa ushered everyone back.

"Okay, Henri, before they get through, light the fuse, and we're off... with luck." This last part he said under his breath.

They all scrambled somewhere safe while their brute tried to get the lighter to work. He flicked and flicked, but got nowhere, so Georges snatched it out of his hand and ignited the flame.

"This takes a little finesse," she said and put the light to the fuse. It spurted and burst and raced away.

"Oh dear, let's adjourn," the Upperlord said, running back to safety with Henri behind her.

The others dragged down a bar of metal as thick as Henri's fist to secure the hefty doors and piled furniture in front for extra protection.

"How long?" Teddy asked, pushing a crate.

"Any moment now," Pa said, standing back with his hands on his hips, his full attention on the entrance. "Any moment."

"They must be through the gate by now," Georges said. "They'll be knocking soon."

A percussive wave split the air and shook the building, sending people to their knees. People screamed and curled on the floor with the rumbling boom of the explosion.

Still shaking from the impact, Teddy accepted Jolon's assistance and got off the ground. They clung to each other not out of fear, but out of shock. He stared at the doors, which were half bent off their hinges.

"Oh, wow."

Teddy agreed with his brother, his ears ringing. "Guess the explosives were still good."

They all cleared the way to the entryway and Henri put his strength into removing the metal bar, now twisted and deformed. Pa and Georges gave him a hand and with much grunting and cursing, the three of them managed to pull it free. As soon as they did, one of the doors fell down with a resounding wham. Ma arched a pale eyebrow as the heavy slab nearly landed on her.

"Sorry, dear," he said with a sheepish grin.

"Hmmm." She strode over to the door to peer outside. Teddy joined her with the others close behind.

Smoke and dust whirled around tainting the air with an acidic tang. Far on the other side, one gate swung with a limp wave until its remaining hinge gave way and tumbled into the cavern too, clanging and thumping its way down. The rest of the structure was gone. They were cut off with no way to build again even if they wanted to. On Belinda's side, the crowd of Uppers and their loyal followers gathered from the places they hid.

"You are a fool, Truman! You condemned yourselves to certain death!"

"And you are an ass, Lindy," Georges replied, coughing from the smoke.

Belinda started to pace, watching the edge as earth and cement still crumbled away. "Always humorous, Georges, always ready to mock. Well, I'm not rescuing you this time. This is your destiny, and when the rest come crawling back for food, water, and air, you needn't bother joining them because you are done."

Georges peered over the edge and grinned. "I don't think there will be any crawling, Lindy. I think you all are on your own now. Luck with getting your hands messy and careful with your suit; it's much too fine to dig through the refuse with. Bye, Lindy." She waved and turned around, stuffing her hands in her pockets and whistling.

Pa laughed and clapped Henri on the back as the two of them went into the warehouse.

Ma hugged Teddy. "Is this place as good as they say?" she whispered in his ear though his head was still ringing, so her voice sounded wobbly. Her fears slipping through her collected countenance.

"Yes, Ma, it's beautiful."

She sighed as she pondered the damage done and the crowd of people staring at them, lost and confused. "It better be."

They went inside, and Henri blocked off the entrance with the old door and a dilapidated cabinet.

"To be extra safe," he said though Teddy couldn't imagine what he expected. Did he think they would cross the expanse with a sudden growth of wings?

"What have you done?" It was Dorkas. How he ended up with them, Teddy didn't know, but it wasn't a good thing.

"Oh, perfect," Caden muttered, coming up behind them. "Out of all the people we left, why couldn't he be one of them?"

Pa climbed high on a counter so he could see everyone. "Easy, everyone, this will all be fine...."

"Fine? Fine! How is this going to be fine? We have nothing!" Dorkas shouted with several others muttering agreement. "I know you, Truman. You never could accept your place. Always had to be better than your superiors, and now you destroyed everything. We have nothing."

"Oh, what'll we do?"

"We'll never survive!"

"We have no food."

"And air, what about air? We'll die!"

The shrieking and shouting climbed in decibels until everyone was close to terror.

"That's not true," Georges answered, getting on the counter with Pa.

It did not surprise Teddy the entire crowd fell silent; they were accustomed to listening to an Upperlord and even one expelled from Upper circles had authority. So they stopped, even Dorkas.

"Okay, we didn't start this without a plan. Yes, we hoped to take a little more time and do this with more stealth. Things got a little out of our control."

"What plan?" Dorkas demanded. A few of his friends muttered along with him.

Georges turned toward Pa and gave an elaborate wave. "Truman, my dear, if you don't mind?"

"Uh, sure," Pa said, a touch flustered.

"Don't fall apart now," she whispered. "If they even doubt for a moment we are unsure of what we're doing, we will be done for."

"Henri, how about we start this move and get these people to paradise?" Pa called out with as much positive energy as he could.

"What paradise?" Dorkas barked.

"There's a whole other city we can live in," Teddy shouted, jumping in. "It's beautiful, even nicer than Uppercity."

"That's impossible."

"The boy lies."

"Where?"

Putting up a hand, Georges caught their attention. "It's true, the boy's right. A while back Tru discovered some tunnels behind his home. We've been exploring them in hopes of finding a better home for everyone. Now, we've found one a few hours' journey from here." She started pacing the length of the table, and Teddy thought it was a good thing she was sober.

"This place has running water...beds...air...." She leaned in as gasps of joy went through the Underlings, "Lights." She nodded as their excitement grew. "That's right. There is a generator, which runs on steam. And plenty of room for everyone!"

A raucous cheer went up, and even Dorkas almost seemed pleased.

"So, when do we go?"

"Let's go now."

"What about food?"

"My dad can't walk."

"Now, calm down, please. We'll leave as soon as we get organized," Georges told them before she motioned to Pa again. "Tru, I think this is where you come in."

"Thanks, Georges, for helping us." They shook hands, and she stepped down, joining Teddy, Jolon, and Ma. "Now, we do have two carts here to assist those who need help. We hoped to have more, but, as Georges said, we ran into some trouble. However, if we work together, we should be able to move in safety."

He motioned to Nuna, who joined him. "This wonderful lady here is Nuna. She and her wife built the generator and were the first people to inhabit the new area. She will be our guide as to what are the best areas for people to live in and what is safe and what isn't. My amazing partner, who you know, and our ever-diligent Mrs. Fish, who knows everyone, will assist her in helping us all settle. Now, if we can get you, Dorkas, and you, Max, and you, Gerard, to meet with us we can get organized for the move. It will take effort to get there, but the road's decent. My kids and I spent the last while getting everything ready."

"We need to repair the stairwell," Caden said, and their father agreed.

"That won't take much with a bit of help." He hopped down from the table, motioning for the others to come with him.

"Not bad. That was clever politics you presented," Ma said to Georges as they went to their home.

She gave her a toothy smile. "Well, sometimes you must get as close to the truth as you can when you have no notion what you're talking about."

"Yeah, guessing—dangerous, but effective," she replied before she turned to everyone else. "You lot go get what you want out of your rooms. Don't take too much, you'll have enough to carry, but you can take a few things. Caden, help Deb. She doesn't understand what's happening, and I need you to keep hold of her."

Teddy started to object. He wanted to be a part of the planning, but she scowled at him, so he trailed after the others and went to his room. There wasn't much he wanted to keep. His journal could go. He stuffed it in a canvas sack he absconded from a junk pile a while back. The box of papers weighed too much to bother with. He snatched up a little container with precious things his parents gave him. After, he rummaged through stuff collected over the years, things he thought were neat or interesting: fascinating pictures and bits of books he read several times. Everything was special, but he left it all.

He swung his hammock back and forth. It never occurred to him he would miss this room, but the space was his, the first place he ever felt secure in since he could remember.

"Is it true, we're leaving?" Deb stood in his doorway with her bear in her hand and a happy-sad expression on her face.

"Yep, we've got a new home."

She stepped in, holding her stuffy tight. "But I like this one."

He knelt in front of her and hugged her. "So do I, but the other one is even more magical. Wait until you see the fountain plaza. That's what Nuna calls it. This huge fountain stands in the centre of the whole place and sparkles as the lights dance over everywhere. There're vast comfy beds and so much more. I can't think of a better place for someone as special as you as this place."

"Any windows?" she asked, her eyes wide.

Grinning, he brushed her hair. "Yes. Some even look out over a forest of trees."

"Trees?" She exhaled, blowing her hair from her eyes. "Do you think we'll see rain?"

The question caught him off guard. He had never thought of the rain. "It's possible, makes sense. You can see clouds."

"Clouds? Will you show me the clouds?"

"Uh, huh," he said, and she smiled with satisfaction. "And will you watch the rain with me?" "All day, if you want."

She thought about this for a moment before she assented. "Fine. I'll go, but I want my room right by yours... well, by yours and Caden's—Jolon too, of course, and Ma shares with Pa, and Henri. I like Henri. He's a good brute."

Teddy laughed. "We'll all be together, don't worry. And he's a fantastic brute."

His sister skipped away to gather up her treasures. He sank into the broken armchair by his desk, his heart heavy.

"Reconsidering?"

He peered up at Caden, and she sat down on the bed beside him. "No, and yes. I guess. We should be excited or happy or something, shouldn't we? We're going to a better place. I know it's a better place. It's real hope for the first time, right?"

"Yeah," she said with a shrug. "Still, I don't know about you, but I didn't picture things going this way."

"What do you mean?"

She waved in the general direction of the warehouse. "Out there are a whole lot of people clinging to the edge of panic. They all trust us to bring them somewhere special. Yet, we're just guessing all will be better. We don't know that for real. And let's not even think about the people still trapped in Undercity. We've left them in the pit with those damn Upperlords."

"Yeah, but we're going to go back and get them," Teddy cut in, frowning at her.

"Are we?" she asked with an expectant gaze. "How? When? Most of those people out there are talking like we're never coming back. They want to seal Undercity away and forget it exists."

"That's just now. They're scared. Once we get settled, they'll see. They'll want to come back and get those we left. And we'll be stronger. The leaching, life-sucking Uppers won't be able to stop us."

She tapped a finger against his leg as she stood. "You keep thinking that."

"You can't be so cynical," he protested. "People aren't all bad."

"No," she said, pausing at the door. "I hope not."

Please, give a Review.

Thanks for joining in on the Undercity adventure. Reviews are the lifeblood of authors. They help indie authors show up better online and allow us to write more books for you. If you enjoyed this story even a little, please leave a review on the website you discovered Undercity on. Thanks.

Keep reading for a preview of book 2 of the Undercity Series

Outside In - Chapter 1

Caden pressed her forehead and hands against the glass and stared out at a world she longed to experience. Green, the word thrived in her brain now. When she closed her eyes at bedtime, she imagined dripping leaves and swaying grasses. All night, she walked among the foliage—touching petals, holding flowers, imagining the feel of the breeze on her skin and the perfume of life in her nose. In the morning, she almost breathed scented air when she woke.

She flattened her palms against the windowpane, part of her wishing the glass would melt and let her out. But tempered panels such as this didn't break easy, according to her brother. Amid the wild greenery outside, crumbled, broken structures poked through like markers of times past. Why some people built their buildings to withstand the disaster, and others didn't, she didn't understand.

Teddy insisted almost a full month passed since their ragged community settled in the tower. She paid little attention to how many days came and went; she just appreciated one more. The transition between their old existence and their new life shocked, in both good and bad ways, the hundred or so people who survived the trip. Life was good; people had water, air, food, and supplies in abundance here. And they had room, lots of room, enough for everyone to use a real bed, to be clean, and to live. Most people adjusted well to the new standard of living though some discovered new levels of greed and lust for more. For others, they hid, cowering and scrounging in the more dilapidated areas as though this was the life they understood and they would face nothing better.

Absently, she removed her headscarf and worked at the twists of her coarse hair, rubbing in the hair oil Pa scrounged up for her. Caden didn't understand. Who thinks of a pleasant room and a comfortable bed as anything evil? She blinked, eyes dry, and continued to stare at the fields and forest below. If they couldn't handle this, how would they ever survive going outside? Her breath caught at the idea. Outside—what a dream. It looked safe, but was it?

"Ma's been looking for you," said an ever-cheerful voice behind her.

She turned and smiled at Deb who sprawled out on her bed on her side of the room. Caden plopped down on her own bed near the window. At first, she didn't want to share a room with her little sister, but after a couple of nights of total silence, she found she couldn't sleep without Deb's mumbling in her sleep.

"I thought you were in Teddy's school. Bored so soon?"

Her sister scrunched her button nose and twirled a strand of blonde hair. They were so different, and not only because Caden was adopted. Deb exuded health and energy with sparkling blue eyes and an eternal smile while her own sable complexion was patchy and scarred. Vitality left her as though she had holes in the bottom of her feet that let everything out. She did not begrudge her little sister any, though; she adored Deb like she was her own, having been with her since she was born. The little girl seemed to understand that no matter how gruff she was she didn't mean to be cranky with anyone. It was a security valve, a safe place to breathe. Any sense of caring terrified her like a long climb up a dilapidated staircase.

Deb went to the window, curling up on the ledge, a mysterious smile on her face. "No. School ended early today. Teddy is still trying to sort out the classes and stuff. He hasn't got enough books, 'n pencils, 'n other things he says he needs. The other kids all went to help out in the sunshine room."

"And you didn't want to go?"

"Nope."

Caden crawled off the bed and tugged on a grey sweater over her burgundy t-shirt. After, she pulled on the boots Pa scrounged for her and tucked her baggy grey pant legs into the tops. "Coming?" she asked as she went to the door.

Her sister shook her head. "Gonna go over to the playroom later."

"Have fun," she said and left the room and went into the hall, which was gloomy despite the smattering of lights that worked. The one thing they did not find many of was light bulbs, particularly the long tube type that seemed to break easily.

As she loped through the passage, she ran her fingers along the wood trim halfway up the wall. Green paper puckered on the walls and peeled away in spots as though tired of holding on. The frantic pattern of the orange and brown rug did little to ease her spirits. A spasm of pain coursed through the middle of her back and up her neck. The tendons in her hands resisted as she flexed them. Little gave way as she massaged her left shoulder, the muscles tight and fingers somewhat numb.

"Ma got a job for you too?" asked Jolon as he met her at the stairs. His soft curls of black hair were shorn tight to his head, making his tawny face seem rounder than ever with his pudgy cheeks and lips. He made up the second youngest in their mismatched family and lived with them for over four years; yet still had not grown an inch upward though he expanded sideways.

Caden patted his head. "Yeah, baldy, nifty cut. You do that to yourself or get cornered by Mrs. Fish and her wayward scissors?"

Jolon stuck out his tongue, his cheeks flushing like apples. "Took a wrong turn and ran into her studying me like I was her next experiment. Would a run, but Pa showed up and thought a trim was a super idea. Trim, right, more like a shearing."

She chuckled as they headed down to the main floor and the table room where her mother made her headquarters. "On the shinier side, now you have less to wash."

"Ha, ha, funny," he huffed and straightened his shirt, tucking the plaid material in his dark pants. "Since we got to this place Ma caught some kinda clean bug. My teeth aren't even safe anymore since they found those little brushes."

They entered the plaza where the massive fountain with the sparkling lights stood. A few people lingered by the entrance to the darker part of the complex, but otherwise, the place was quiet. The new settlement was a maze of interconnected tunnels and buildings with many areas yet to be explored. Caden preferred to keep to the familiar areas, scrounging no longer holding her interest.

"Yeah, they took all my favourite clothes away the other day. Even my purple sweater right when it reached the right level of comfort and wear."

"Meh, I hid mine," her brother said, his hands jammed in his pockets and forehead wrinkled. "No one is gettin' anything more from me that I don't want to give up."

Caden grinned at him and spied a familiar figure by the fountain.

"Hey, there's Cate," she said, waving to the girl sitting on the fountain's ledge, her arm in the water. Her coils of rusty hair almost touched the rippled surface of the pool as she strained to get whatever held her attention. Grime streaked her face and stained her ragged shirt while a long brown belt cinched her baggy grey pants to her waist.

"You're gonna fall in if you bend over anymore," Caden said as they came up beside her. She smiled at her long-time friend who came from the same dark place in Undercity she grew up in. Unlike Caden, who, despite her hunched shoulders, was tall and never kept on any weight. Her friend was solid in build like she hoarded muscles in case of a shortage. Short and stocky described her best, but she had an engaging smile when coaxed out of her. Other differences went deeper than physical. Both had weaknesses, which left them scrambling to survive. Cate trusted no one or anything enough to be comfortable in a community. Fierce in her independence, she stayed in the darker part of the mall with the other hiders, so finding her out in the center of everything surprised Caden.

She nudged Cate on the leg. "Here, let me help. My long arms gotta be useful sometimes."

The other girl screwed up her face in a frown, but sat up, shaking her dripping arm. Her hair covered half her face and hid her empty eye socket from sight.

"Fine. Get the marble in that corner." She gestured to a large blue stone under the surface.

"That piece of glass, what do you want that for?" Jolon asked in his usual forthright manner.

Cate glared at him with her one grey-blue eye. "That's none of your business."

Jolon shrugged as though he didn't care. "Wonderful to see moving hasn't changed everything," he grumbled as he glared back. "Meet you at the kitchens, Caden." He shuffled off in his plodding way.

"You could get along with him," Caden suggested as she knelt over the fountain and reached for the stone.

"You get along with him. I think he's a blob," her friend retorted as she waited, her teeth working over her bottom lip. She picked up a teacup filled with candle wax resting on the edge of the fountain and stared at the tiny flame flickered in the center.

"Pretty. Where'd you find that?" Caden asked, nodding toward the candle.

Cate ran a finger around the rim. "Made it. Found a bunch of broken candles and some cups. Thought they'd work well together, so I melted the wax, and there you go."

Caden grinned. "Clever."

"Beats stumbling in the dark," she said with a shrug and a small smile.

"Yeah, don't miss that," Caden said, remembering the times when they huddled together in the dirt and darkness, making cutting remarks about everything around them. Every morning they would wake up to gnawing hunger and shivering cold. The rest of the time they scrounged for scraps and hid in the shadows to avoid unwanted attention.

When Caden's adoptive parents took her in, they offered to help Cate too, but she didn't trust anyone. Even though the years proved their hearts and actions true, it was as if Cate thought happiness was impossible for her. She visited Caden, but avoided the rest of the family.

Caden captured the glass ball in her fingers, her right hand joints complaining against the cold. "Here you are," she said with a smile, and held the little orb up. "Nice."

Cate took the stone and clutched it in close as though she thought someone would snag the treasure from her. "Yeah, found it in a shop. Thought the size was about right..." she stopped, clamping her lips shut and avoiding Caden's gaze.

"Good scrounge," Caden said, knowing better than to press. As she got up and put a hand through her hair. "Well, I gotta go, but we could get together later?" She tried not to make her words sound like a plea, but she missed her friend like she would miss half of herself.

The other girl made a derisive gesture as she got up. "I'm sure you'll have other things to do."

Caden caught her arm. "I won't. And if I do, you can join me."

"What, and obey?" she mocked with a hollow laugh. "Sure, I can mince along like you."

The words took her off guard. She released her hold and Cate hurried away. Her friend disappeared into the shadows of the undeveloped part of the mall. A heavy sigh escaped from Caden's lips as she rose and straightened her stiff back. Confused, she pushed all thoughts of Cate aside before shuffling toward the kitchen. Instinctively, she hunched and cast her eyes downward upon entering the table room, her usual stance when confronted by a room full of people. The space was huge with only a few survivors around, but they still scared her. Teddy sat at a table with several girls and guys around their age. Since the move, her brother became popular. Many painted him and Pa as heroes, which irked like a pinprick in the side. Somehow tower residents forgot her part as though she wasn't present when they discovered a way to paradise.

"Hey," Teddy called as he sauntered over. Several of those vying for his attention rolled their eyes at her, but he showed no interest in them. He changed a little in the last couple of months. His clothes were tidy and his smile ever ready, but he still had circles under his eyes from late nights with books and writing. His chestnut hair still hung in a mess. However, he appeared older now, taller and more square, his khaki tinted face more angular.

"Hey, yourself," she answered back with a grimace and a nod to the crowd behind them. "Your fandom is growing."

"My what?" He glanced behind him. "Oh, ahh, they're searching for something to do. It's funny, before we kept busy surviving and now pickings are so easy everyone seems lost." He nodded toward her, his hands stuffed in his pocket and shoulders slouched.

She never realized he and Jolon had the same habit before. Which one picked the quirk up from the other, she couldn't guess.

"You going to visit Ma?" he continued as he fell in step with her.

"Yep. She probably has some weird new recipe for me to try out."

They left via a swinging door and went along a walkway with a cement floor and dirty walls. Tables and carts lined one side, narrowing the aisle. The path turned left at the end and opened to a noisy kitchen of shouting cooks and their drudges. Pots and pans banged and swung about while knives flicked over root vegetables. Overhead, lights flickered from power fluctuations. Mrs. Fish waved at them from her station by the stove, and they nodded at a few more people while making their way to the back room where their mother worked.

"Close the door," Ma ordered as they came in. She sat at a desk covered in papers and books; her wild pale hair tied in a neat bun and her boney face flushed. Her narrow fingers flipped through pages as though she searched for the answers to life's problems.

"What to do, what to do," she muttered. She slammed shut the book in her hands and shook her head at them. "I am amazed at the variety of food people made in the past, so many meals. Stretches the imagination to think of them. Pasta, stews, salad, the variety of ingredients alone is staggering." A smile spread over her face. She was lord of her domain, creating meals out of whatever she could cook.

"Something interesting for supper tonight, Ma?" her brother asked.

"Doubtful," she said with a sigh. "But it'll still be good." She reclined in her chair and put her feet up on her desk, stretching her arms behind her. The folds of her long skirt fell back and revealed her knee-length, black socks and worn runners. "Tired," she yawned. "Need to start a cooking rotation, train some of the others to take over. Then I could take one of those long soaks I keep hearing about without anyone running in on me 'cause the soup's burning."

"Isn't Nuna helping?" Teddy asked.

Ma shrugged at the mention of the original inhabitant of the towers. "The sudden influx of all these people has overwhelmed her somewhat. She doesn't come around too often. Nuna informed me in our last conversation that it was the Peterson family," she waved a hand at all of them, "who wanted to help everyone, so it was the Peterson family who could sort out all the details. Not so nice, I know, but I think she'll come around once everything settles. She had been alone for quite a long time."

Caden played with a little statue of a duck on her mother's desk. "Deb said you wanted me for something."

"Yes, Henri is watching the tunnel, and he must be hungry by now. You and your brothers bring him that box of food." She gestured to a cardboard box by the door.

"The load's not so big, Ma, I don't think this task will take three of us," Caden objected, sensing an ulterior motive.

Their brute brought her flowers every day when they lived in the warehouse. When they moved, he started bringing her everything he thought she might want from different stores. At first, his attention annoyed and frightened her. No one had ever been sweet on her before, and she doubted anyone ever would again. Then she found it wonderful for the same reasons. Now, she was miffed and tired because he did nothing else. He didn't like to talk much, or read, or even hold hands. He gave her things and mooned over her from afar. So she avoided him even though her mother thought they made a wonderful match and liked to promote the idea whenever possible.

Her mother wagged a digit her way and held out a list. "Go with your brothers and gather these ingredients. They're mostly spices and dried teas. Your pa said to check a couple of the stores listed."

Teddy took the list from her. "Sure, Ma. Will do."

Caden remained silent, but her mother narrowed her gaze and gave her a slight nod and a grin. Caden got the message. Sighing, she left with Teddy who took the crate on his way out. Jolon was leaning against one counter, munching on slices of raw potato.

"To the mall, mates," he said with a potato salute.

"To the mall," Teddy agreed with a jaunty grin.

Caden tried to match their relaxed camaraderie, but found her wary nature blocking her way. A hollow ache, worse than hunger, sat in her stomach. Yes, life was better now, but she longed for more.

Teddy put the food on a small cart and pulled it behind him as they left. "Let's go the back way through the halls and out into the lobby."

Jolon chuckled. "Tired of your fans?"

"He's afraid they'll follow us in a parade with banners and such," Caden added, winking at Jolon.

"Funny, so funny," Teddy retorted. "It's faster; that's all."

They both nodded in false agreement, grinning at him. He ignored them and kept going. Their cart rattled across the grey and blue tiles as they went. They passed the central desk and climbed the steps leading to Henri. People milled about, sifting through the ransacked shops.

"There's not too much left that's useful on this level," Teddy told them as they went by store after store. Soon, the place emptied until they were among the few people left.

A person or two made their home in some of the stalls, draping the entrances and windows with strips of cloth and blankets. The dull glow of meagre flickering lights lit their way. Most of the lights no longer worked, and those that did were lengths apart.

It took a while to get back to the area where they first discovered their new home. When they arrived, they found Henri pouring over a book. He looked up as they approached, his massive posture embarrassed as he tucked the book behind his back.

"Oh, uh, hi," he muttered with an odd wave. The move did not change him at all. He was still lumpy muscular with thin brown hair and a hopeful grin on his ash face. He didn't stink so much though.

"Hey," she responded with a shy nod. The expectation of a romantic relationship was irritating. Why couldn't they be friends?

Jolon sat on a bin next to him. "You taking up reading?" He grunted as Teddy ran the cart into him. "Hey, careful."

"He's trying to tell you it's supposed to be a secret," Caden whispered to Jolon and shook her head. "Why hide it, Henri?"

He twitched a bashful shrug. "Dunno."

The brute took on such an uncomfortable expression she let the matter go. "Well, we've brought you some food. Ma sent enough for a dozen people, so this should last you for a few hours. How long are you posted here?"

He shrugged again and took the box. "'Till night." A stiff grin spread across his face. "Thanks."

This time, she shrugged. "Gotta feed ya. Who would protect us otherwise?"

Henri chuckled and took something from behind his back. "For you."

Caden took the shiny black kitty figurine and tried to smile back. "Thanks."

Teddy leaned against one of the cement boulders blocking the access to their new home. "Any action?"

"Nope," Henri answered as he sunk his teeth into a potatocake.

"Doubt there would be." Jolon stuffed a cushion under his backside. "Even if they managed to cross the bridge, it would be a miracle if they found this place after we hid the entrance so well."

"Do you honestly think any of them would bother?" she asked.

"Bother what?" Teddy asked.

She found a plastic crate to sit on and rested her legs. The walk caused the ache to come back, so she rubbed her calves. "Bother trying to get to us. I mean, what's the point? Now, there are less of them to provide for, but they still have enough Underlings to dig for them. Why bother seeking what is gone?"

"I figure they think we're all dead," Jolon added.

Teddy frowned. "Georges doesn't think so. She figures they believe we found something better than what they possess, and they want it. She says they probably met with each other and talked themselves into a frenzy of selfishness and revenge, so we should keep a vigilant eye on everywhere."

Georges, Caden sniffed at the mention of the strange Upperlord with the cynical intelligence and apathetic demeanour.

"They removed her title."

Caden arched an eyebrow at Teddy. "Why? What does a title matter here?"

Her brother shrugged. "Dorkas threw a fit and got everyone riled up."

"He's good at that."

"Yeah, well, he convinced the other elders that as long as Georges held a title she would always be above everyone; therefore, everyone else would always defer to her."

She laughed at this. "Yes, because that's what Dorkas wants. While Georges holds such a distinction, Dorkas can't."

"That's ridiculous, true, but ridiculous." Jolon brushed dirt from his trousers, his expression one of bored annoyance.

"Why want title? Just words," said Henri, who finished eating half his food and put the rest away on a corner table near his chair.

"It's not just the words," Teddy explained. "It's the power that goes with them. Now that Dorkas discovered all this place offers, he wants more."

"Jolon right, that red... redicu... ridiculous."

"Especially since our community consists of only, what, a couple hundred of us?" said Caden. She stretched her arms above her head as her back seized. "What's the point of lording over anyone?"

"Some people like power," Teddy said, and Caden guessed by his blank face his mind flitted back to the stories he read.

The discovery of the shops led to a whole new world of resources for Teddy's insatiable appetite for reading and knowledge. Though Caden never enjoyed reading—the lines always seemed to get away from her—she did love to listen. Often, in the evenings, he would read to her and the others stories from his new books or something he scratched out himself. It was a good ritual. She liked rituals. They made her feel safe, consistent within such boundaries. The greatest difficulty she found adjusting to their new home was the departure from everything familiar. Though all their rooms were clustered together, they no longer had a common space for only their family. Nor did they catch each other as they were going by. Now the doors were always closed, and she had to knock to gain access. Not that that was too hard, but it seemed more intrusive—separated and distant. They ate at the same table, but in a horde of people. They gathered in the common area, and others joined them. It was both crowded and lonely.

"We should head back," Teddy decided as he stood.

"Yeah," Jolon said with a dramatic weary stretch as though hard labour awaited him.

"Go now?" Henri asked, his open face tragic. He got up and gazed at Caden with hopeful puppy eyes.

She managed an awkward smile and rose to her feet. "We'll talk to you later, Henri. Ma always has stuff for us to do and Deb wanders off."

He slumped in the shoulders and nodded. "K."

They left him and headed back in silence for most of the way. Everyone wanted her to like Henri, and she did, but not like Ma liked Pa and vice versa. Love and intimacy like that confused and scared her.

The Chaos Continues:

Thanks for your support.
Connect with us at:
www.juliettestudios.com
Twitter: @juliettestudios
Instagram: @juliettestudios

About the Author

K ris Moger – The words and ideas.
        Like many creative people, Kris Moger doesn't like writing
bios, but she got talked into it this time. On an average day, she likes to
write, draw, and daydream. On most days, she cleans house, gets distracted, and procrastinates. She has created stories since she was young,
but only started writing them down in the last dozen years. After pub-
lishing a couple of short stories, 'Down and Out' is her first official pub-
lished novel.

Main Cast of Undercity: Down and Out

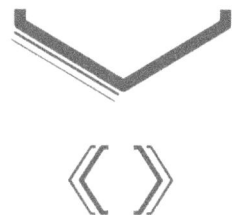

Teddy – Second oldest child of Peterson family

- Eyes – brown
- Hair – chestnut
- Complexion – Khaki
- Build – slight

Caden – Oldest child of Peterson family

- Eyes – amber
- Hair – black twists
- Complexion – sepia brown
- Build – tall, boney

Jolon – Middle child of Peterson family

- Eyes – mud brown
- Hair – curly black

- Complexion – copper
- Build – thick

Deb - youngest child of Peterson family

- Eyes – pale blue
- Hair – light blond
- Complexion – ivory
- Build – slight

Mr. Truman Peterson

- Eyes – pale blue
- Hair – black and grey
- Complexion – drywall grey
- Build – boney

Mrs. Tisha Peterson

- Eyes – grey
- Hair – frizzy blonde
- Complexion – drywall grey
- Build – tall

Henri – brute for Peterson family

- Eyes – forest green

- Hair – thin / dusky brown
- Complexion – freckled white
- Build – slight

Georges – Upperlord and Brute Merchant

- Eyes – gold
- Hair – black and grey braids
- Complexion – coal black
- Build – boney

Belinda – Upperlord and Brute Merchant

- Eyes – gold
- Hair – black braids and twists
- Complexion – coal black
- Build – full-figured

Mrs. Fish – Friend of Peterson family

- Eyes – gold
- Hair – mahogany
- Complexion – tawny
- Build – tall / physically fit

Mr. Fish – Friend of Peterson family

- Eyes – brown
- Hair – black
- Complexion – copper with beard
- Build – brawn

Dorkas – Fellow Underling

- Eyes – grey
- Hair – grey
- Complexion – grey
- Build – narrow

Nuna – Tower Resident

- Eyes – brown
- Hair – chestnut
- Complexion – rusty
- Build – solid